Doctor in Rags

Books by Louise A. Vernon

Title	Subject
The Beggars' Bible	John Wycliffe
The Bible Smuggler	William Tyndale
Doctor in Rags	Paracelsus and Hutterites
A Heart Strangely Warmed	John Wesley
Ink on His Fingers	Johann Gutenberg
Key to the Prison	George Fox and Quakers
The King's Book	King James Version, Bible
The Man Who Laid the Egg	Erasmus
Night Preacher	Menno Simons
Peter and the Pilgrims	English Separatists, Pilgrims
The Secret Church	Anabaptists
Thunderstorm in Church	Martin Luther

Doctor in Rags

Louise A. Vernon
Illustrated by Allan Eitzen

Herald Press

Scottdale, Pennsylvania
Waterloo, Ontario

Library of Congress Cataloging-in-Publication Data

Vernon, Louise A.
   Doctor in Rags.

   SUMMARY: In sixteenth-century Moravia amid persecution of the Hutterites, a twelve-year-old boy influenced by the famous physician, Paracelsus, chooses his vocation.
   [1. Hutterite Brethren—Fiction] I. Eitzen, Allan, illus. II. Title.
PZ7.V598Do   [Fic]   72-5367

The paper used in this publication is recycled and meets the minimum requirements of American National Standard for Information Sciences—Permanence of Paper for Printed Library Materials, ANSI Z39.48-1984.

DOCTOR IN RAGS
Copyright © 1973 by Herald Press, Scottdale, Pa. 15683
   Published simultaneously in Canada by Herald Press,
   Waterloo, Ont. N2L 6H7. All rights reserved
Library of Congress Catalog Card Number: 72-5367
International Standard Book Number: 0-8361-1698-4
Printed in the United States of America

10 09 08 07 06 05 04 03 02 10 9 8 7 6 5 4 3

To order or request information, please call
1-800-759-4447 (individuals); 1-800-245-7894 (trade).
Website: www.mph.org.

Contents

1. Strangers at the Gate /7
2. Terror in the Village /18
3. Unpleasant Surprise /31
4. Secret Medicine /45
5. Buried Treasure /58
6. A Bitter Pill /70
7. Preacher Out of Church /80
8. Mysterious Message /92
9. Sharing and Caring /103
10. The Swiss Brethren /115
11. Trial of Faith /125
12. Mission from God /136

1
Strangers at the Gate

The gate bell jangled outside the walled courtyard of a small castle near a mountain village in Moravia. Twelve-year-old Michael Bruhn heard the bell and rushed upstairs to the sickroom of his ten-year-old sister Gudryn.

"Mother," he called in a loud whisper, "the doctor is here."

His mother came to the door of the sickroom. "The doctor? Impossible!" she exclaimed. "I sent the messenger just this morning. Even if he galloped all the way, he couldn't have reached the city this soon. Michael," she went on, "I've warned you before about being so impulsive. Find out the truth before you speak."

Michael sighed. Mother was right. He should have checked with the gatekeeper instead of making a wild guess.

"I'll go see who it is," he offered, and started toward the balcony overlooking the courtyard.

"Wait!" Mother's voice sounded choked. "I'm afraid it's --" Her voice trailed off.

Michael stared at his mother in astonishment. Not once since his father's death two months before had Mother used the word "afraid." Her firm belief in God's mercy never wavered. What could she be afraid of? A tiny chill of forewarning, like an icy finger, ran down Michael's spine.

Old Leonard, a trusted family servant, hurried up the main staircase. Before he could speak, Mother called out, "Have they come?"

A puzzled expression crossed Leonard's wrinkled face. "They? I do not know who Madame means, but I do know there is a traveler on horseback at the gate. He insists on speaking with you."

"A traveler?" Mother echoed, relieved. "You know our custom, Leonard. Offer him food in God's name and send him on his way."

"But Madame, this man is different." Leonard wrung his hands in his effort to explain. "He's not a peasant. Still, his words are rough and unpolished. And his clothes --" Leonard looked down his long nose and shuddered with distaste. "His clothes are just rags."

"A traveler doesn't wear satin or velvet," Mother suggested with a slight smile.

"No, Madame, of course not. But this man is unlike anyone I've ever seen."

Michael could not curb his curiosity. "What makes him different?"

Old Leonard thought a moment. "Perhaps it's his piercing eyes."

"Is he old or young?"

"Not so young, with his puff of white hair around a high, bald forehead. Still, he wears no beard, and he stutters like a gawky youth, but his words are like a wise man's." Leonard clasped his hands in appeal. "Will Madame speak with him?"

"Of course not." Mother dismissed him.

In a little while, Leonard came back, his face aglow with excitement. "Madame, you must see him. He can heal your young daughter lying there so ill."

Mother's lips tightened into a firm line. "I have sent for one of the best doctors in Moravia to attend Gudryn."

Leonard's wrinkled face twitched with mixed emotions. "But Madame," he cried out, "this man is the best doctor in the whole world. The servants say he is Paracelsus."

"Paracelsus? What an odd name. Just who is this Paracelsus?"

"He's a doctor."

"A doctor? In rags? Ridiculous. He's probably no more than a barber-surgeon from the village."

Barber-surgeons, as Michael knew, had little or no medical training, but poor people could not afford qualified doctors.

"Madame, he's more than a barber-surgeon."

Michael could see that Leonard was determined not to give up. Since Father's death, the old man had been more of a friend than a servant in helping Mother with the problems of the estate. "His cures are miracles," Leonard continued. "He treats rich and poor; he doesn't care which, just so he can help the patient get well. He even reads the Bible to his patients, and if they are too poor to buy one, he gives them one free."

"Leonard, that is enough." Mother was firm. "He sounds like a fine man, but I have already sent for a doctor. Tell this Paracelsus so at once."

"Yes, Madame," Leonard bowed and left.

A little later the gate bell sounded. Michael impulsively headed for the balcony.

"Wait, Michael."

For the second time that day, Michael heard Mother's unspoken fear.

"I -- I want you to look after your sister for a while."

Michael did not object to taking care of Gudryn, but his curiosity almost overwhelmed him. What was Mother trying to keep secret?

In Gudryn's room, the curtains of the huge, four-poster bed had been drawn back. His sister lay with eyes closed. A maidservant patted Gudryn's flushed forehead with a soft white cloth. Mother sent the maid to the basement kitchen for hot broth and pulled up the bedclothes to Gudryn's chin.

"Be sure she doesn't throw off the bedcovers.

She has been very restless and shouldn't be left alone even for a minute."

Michael nodded. He hoped his sister would get well fast. She was always good company with her lively, mischievous ways.

"What are you going to do, Mother?" Michael hoped Mother would not notice his intense curiosity.

"I'm going to the gate."

Mother tried to sound matter-of-fact, as if she went to the gate every time the bell rang, but Michael heard the fear again. Her back stiff with determination, she marched downstairs, leaving Michael really alarmed. He looked at Gudryn, now asleep. What harm would it do if he left her for just a minute? He didn't want to see Mother afraid of anything or anybody. He was old enough now to help her, but he would have to know what was going on. Who was at the gate?

Michael ran to the balcony and looked across the courtyard. Through the partly opened gates he saw a group of bearded men in knee-length trousers, short pleated coats with full sleeves, and notched collars. Their wide-brimmed hats had tall, sloping crowns. Michael had never before seen so many strangers at their gate. The men moved quietly, almost gently. How could they be dangerous? Yet if Mother were afraid, why did she permit the gates to be opened?

A thump sounded from Gudryn's room. With a guilty start, Michael rushed back. Gudryn lay motionless on the floor, bedclothes tumbled all around her. Horrified, he tugged at her limp hand.

"Gudryn, get back in bed," he urged.

His sister's eyelids fluttered. She moaned and tried to sit up. "I can't move my legs."

Michael put his hands under her arms and tugged, but her legs were a dead weight. Perspiration beaded his forehead. Why had he left her? Would she be all right? With a desperate heave, he helped her onto the bed.

"What were you trying to do, Gudryn?" he panted.

"I woke up and nobody was here, so I tried to get up," she explained. "Now my legs feel numb."

"It's all my fault," Michael reproached himself again and again.

Later, after Gudryn drifted off to sleep, Michael heard his mother and Leonard talking in the hall.

"Did Madame send for a Hutterite doctor?"

Michael heard strong disapproval in the old servant's voice.

"No, Leonard. I sent for a doctor from the city."

"But these men I saw Madame talking to just now are Hutterites. Why are they here?"

"I arranged yesterday for them to come," Mother said.

"But Madame knows the law." Leonard's voice rose in dismay.

"Someone has to plant the crops and harvest them. How else can we raise taxes for King Ferdinand?"

"Madame cannot be so foolish as to allow Hutterites to build a Bruderhof on this estate."

Michael tried to remember what he had heard about the Hutterites. Weren't they people who had broken away from the church? Hadn't King Ferdinand ordered them to be hunted and punished by exile or death? Even if an innocent person like Mother even talked to Hutterites, she could be punished. A strange, nameless fear choked Michael. Mother was breaking the law. What would happen to her -- and to Michael and Gudryn? He moved closer to the door and listened.

"Leonard, do you have any idea of what a Bruderhof is?" Mother asked.

"I know the Hutterites live together like one family. They build themselves a big house to live in, and they all eat together in one big room, and --"

"And worship together," Mother interrupted. "Have you heard that?"

"Yes, Madame," Leonard admitted.

"They educate their children, both boys and girls, even children who aren't Hutterites," Mother went on. "Did you know that?"

"No, Madame. But why should girls be educated?" Leonard asked.

"So they can read the Bible and worship God."

Leonard mumbled something Michael couldn't hear.

"Leonard, you haven't forgotten how Michael's

tutor fled with the field workers two months ago?"

"That was because of the plague scare, Madame. People were afraid your husband died of it, but even so, that's no reason to bring in Hutterites. Madame knows very well that for three years now, ever since 1534, it has been against the law to hire them."

Michael listened, perplexed. A new thought bothered him. Why would Mother, of all people, deliberately break the law?

"Other estate owners allow Bruderhofs to be built," Mother said. "Besides, the king doesn't have enough soldiers to take over every estate in Moravia." She added, "I have given the Hutterites permission to build a Bruderhof on this estate. They worship God in the right way."

So that was why Mother dared to break the law!

For the third time that afternoon, the gate bell pealed. From the excited scrambling of servants in the lower hall, Michael knew the doctor must have arrived. A man in a red, fur-lined cloak and fur-lined hat ascended the steps. He clasped a gold walking stick with a white-gloved hand. A silver-tipped dagger glittered at his side.

An assistant in short cloak, yellow scarf, and velvet cap trotted behind the doctor. The doctor and his assistant entered the sickroom and closed the door. For a long time there was no sound; then the door was flung open. The doctor beckoned Michael.

"Your mother tells me you will run an errand for me. Go to the apothecary in the village and get the medicine I ordered."

The command bothered Michael. Why would a doctor order medicine before he knew what the illness was?

"Who were those men waiting by the gate?" the doctor asked in forceful tones.

Startled out of his thoughts, Michael blurted, "They're Hutterites." He could have bitten his tongue. Why hadn't he thought before he spoke? What if the doctor told the city officials? Michael tried not to think of the terrible trouble his hasty remark could cause.

The doctor raised his eyebrows but said nothing. His assistant came out of the sickroom. "About this child -- would bloodletting help?"

The doctor snorted in scorn. "Just like a first-year medical student! Bloodletting is for the village barber-surgeon, but not for a doctor worthy of his hat. It won't help a paralysis." He lowered his voice. "Nothing will. This girl will never walk again, but we'll stay for a while and collect a handsome fee."

Michael stared at the doctor in angry disbelief. Gudryn not walk again? It couldn't be true! This doctor wanted only money. He didn't care at all about his patient.

Sick at heart, Michael started downstairs. Why, oh, why had he been so impulsive? If he had stayed by Gudryn's bed, she wouldn't have fallen.

Now she was paralyzed. How could he undo the trouble he had caused? He tried to pray, but the words stuck in his throat. Maybe he could ask the Hutterites how they prayed.

Two maidservants scurried past. "Did you hear? Madame's daughter is paralyzed. What a sorrowful thing for her to face after the death of her husband."

"If you ask me, Madame has tempted God," the second maidservant retorted. "Did you know she's letting the Hutterites build a Bruderhof here? It's against the law. Hutterite doctors, though -- that's a different story. Everyone knows how good they are. Even the king has had a Hutterite doctor."

Michael paused, his hand on the stair railing. Sudden hope sprang up in him. Why not find a Hutterite doctor for Gudryn?

He crossed the courtyard. Outside the gates a few Hutterites clustered around a man clothed in a dirty, ragged, fur-lined coat and a battered fur-lined hat. The man was beardless, with a high, bald forehead and wisps of white hair. He kept one hand on the pommel of an enormous sword at his side and held the leading rope of his horse in his other hand. Saddlebags on the horse almost burst with pots, surgical instruments, and rolls of charts.

"God is the first physician," Michael heard him tell the Hutterites. "Call not for help to man, but ask it from God acting through man, and He will send you the physician, or He may aid you through the p-p-power within yourself, provided you are holy or a physician yourself."

When the man turned, Michael felt the burn of his piercing eyes. This man was the doctor in rags!

"L-l-let God be the highest and first physician. Nothing takes place without Him."

Michael strained to hear every word. He could have listened forever to this compelling man who, in his earnestness, sometimes stuttered. A doctor working with God could cure Gudryn! Michael had never felt so sure of anything in his life. But how could he persuade Mother?

2

Terror in the Village

Michael lingered near the gate, knowing he should hurry to the village for the medicine the city doctor had ordered for Gudryn. But who could trust a doctor who ordered medicine before he had examined the patient?

Michael edged closer to the Hutterites. Before he could gather enough courage to speak to Paracelsus, an armed horseman rode up.

"Are you the Hutterites?"

A chilled silence fell over the group. Michael felt like a Hutterite himself. Here was danger! The horseman might be a spy hired by the king to discover suspected heretics. If the Hutterites

The armed horseman asked, "Are you the Hutterites?"

admitted who they were, arrest, exile, and even death might follow, all because they determined to follow God's will at whatever the cost. These hunted people had to overcome their natural fear by faith in God, but no Hutterite could be expected to betray himself to an enemy.

Paracelsus answered for the Hutterites. "Why do you ask?"

The horseman drew back from Paracelsus' rough speech and ragged clothes but answered politely. "My father, the count, is ill, and I am looking for a Hutterite doctor."

"Are Hutterite doctors exempt from being arrested?" Paracelsus asked.

"I am not betraying any Hutterites to the king's men, if that's what you're afraid of," the horseman answered. "My father is ill, and he has consulted many doctors. They have all given up. I don't want any more city doctors who insist on high fees and the finest of food at the family table, but do nothing to help the patient."

"Sham-physicians!" Paracelsus snorted. "They know how to wear the doctor's garb, and how to shine among the ignorant like dirt in a lantern, but the slaughter they achieve among the sick is worse than that by a warrior in the trenches."

The horseman smiled at this outburst. "I want a good doctor, either a Hutterite or someone like the famed Paracelsus."

Laughter rippled among the Hutterites. The horseman frowned.

"I am Paracelsus," the doctor in rags said in his rough accent.

"You?" the horseman gasped. "You don't look like a doctor or sound like one either."

"I am different," Paracelsus admitted, "but let this not upset you. My speech may be rough, but it's the language of my own country, and at Einsiedeen, in Switzerland, where I grew up, people don't learn polite manners and refined language."

"But I have heard your cures are miracles. Your fame has spread all over the continent."

Michael understood what the horseman was really saying. If Paracelsus was such a success, why did he wear such ragged clothes?

Paracelsus must have understood this, too. He gestured toward the overflowing saddlebags on his horse. "A doctor should be a wayfarer."

The explanation seemed to convince the horseman. "Will you come with me?"

For answer, Paracelsus mounted his horse. The two men started off.

"I think my father has a blood disease," Michael heard the horseman say.

With his usual vigor, Paracelsus retorted, "A blood disease? How do you know it is the blood's fault? There are as many kinds of blood as there are trees in the wood."

When the men left, there was nothing for Michael to do but go to the village apothecary and get the medicine for Gudryn. At the village, he climbed a steep street to the apothecary's shop and found it empty. Jars of all shapes stood jammed together on the shelves, and a strong odor of a bitter herb stung his eyes.

"Hello," Michael called. He heard no reply.

"Anybody here?" he called again.

"Downstairs," a boy's voice answered.

Michael walked back to a narrow stairway. Hot, smoky air drifted up from the cellar.

The unseen boy called out, "Just a minute. I have to wait for this to boil."

Michael went part way down the stairs. He saw a boy about his own age crouching by a fire at one corner. He held a long-handled pan over the flames until the liquid boiled, then placed the pan on two stones and let a few drops of the liquid slide off a wooden spoon. They spun a thread, and the boy grunted with satisfaction.

"Hello. What are you doing?" Michael spoke louder than he intended. Somehow the smoke made him feel he had to fight it.

Startled, the other boy jerked around, knocking the pan over. The liquid seethed, hissed, and disappeared.

Michael apologized.

"Oh, well, I was just experimenting."

Michael introduced himself. "I'm Michael Bruhn. Is the apothecary here?"

"He's home. He's very, very ill." The boy added, "My name is Karl Gunter."

"I'm supposed to get some medicine the doctor

ordered," Michael explained.

Karl brightened. "You mean Dr. von Hohenheim?"

"I didn't hear what his name is, but anyway, he said he left an order here."

"Oh, yes. I know the one you mean -- the city doctor." Karl stressed the word "city" with scorn. He took down a small, sealed jar from a cellar shelf. "Here it is. I made it up myself."

"You did?"

Michael's respectful tone brought a fleeting smile to Karl's lips. "It was nothing -- or next to nothing."

Karl's disdain bothered Michael. Surely, a doctor had to know a great deal before he ordered medicines.

Karl went on. "These city doctors order a prescription like that and charge the patient twenty times what it costs."

"What's in it?"

"Flavored sugar water. Imagine!"

Hot anger flared inside Michael. Gudryn needed more than sugar water to cure her paralysis. If only Mother would dismiss the city doctor and ask Paracelsus to cure her -- with God's help!

"Sometimes I think that's why my master is ill," Karl continued. "He's honest. Even Dr. von Hohenheim admits that, and he usually has no use at all for apothecaries."

"Are you going to be an apothecary?"

"No. I'm going to be a doctor."

Karl's matter-of-fact assurance kindled Michael's imagination. The idea of being a doctor excited him.

"How do you start being a doctor?"

"Dr. von Hohenheim says you can start anywhere. The patients are your textbooks, and the sickbed is your study hall. But I'm going to do as he did and travel from school to school in Germany and Italy and all around."

"How will you get there?" Michael asked.

Karl laughed. "Walk, mostly."

"Why can't I be a doctor, too?" Michael asked himself. "You must have to have a lot of money," he said aloud.

"Not if you're a medical student," Karl replied. "You wear a yellow scarf and a student's cap and people feed you or take you in."

Michael felt more and more drawn to the idea of being a doctor. "How did you find all this out?"

"From Dr. von Hohenheim. He came to the town where I used to live -- Sterzing -- when there was a plague. People were leaving town, running away, not even helping the sick ones. Dr. von Hohenheim came and helped everyone, rich or poor. The townspeople thought he was in league with the devil because he saved so many lives, and they ran him out of town." Karl clenched his fists. "My parents died later, and I came here to be an apprentice."

Michael tried to absorb all this information.

Somehow, Dr. von Hohenheim did not sound like the usual city doctor. "Does this doctor wear his fine clothes and white gloves when he is treating people?"

Karl burst out laughing. "Absolutely not. Dr. von Hohenheim travels so much and is só busy doctoring sick people and making their medicines -- he makes his own, mostly -- and writing books, he hasn't time to buy the clothes he needs."

"But his name isn't von Hohenheim. It's Paracelsus," Michael exclaimed.

Karl shook his head. "His name is Theophrastus Bombastus von Hohenheim. He writes books and makes his own medicines. His father was a doctor, too."

Someone called from the front of the shop. "Karl! Karl Gunter!"

Karl's face paled. "It's the village priest. I know what he's going to tell me, and I don't want to hear it." Nevertheless, he went upstairs. Michael followed.

"Karl, I have bad news." The priest announced the apothecary's death, and left to tell the town crier. In a little while the town crier was ringing his bell and shouting the news through the village streets.

"What will you do now?" Michael asked.

"I don't know. I don't have a home."

"Where have you been living?"

Karl nodded toward the back of the shop. "In the cellar." He bolted the shop door and leaned against the counter with his head down. "I feel sick."

Michael heard a shuffling sound outside, like dry leaves before a wind. Voices murmured, rose and fell, until one word began to be repeated in angry tones. "Plague."

Fists hammered on the door. "Burn the shop! It's plague infected." "Where's the boy? Send the plague carrier away." "It's God's punishment. Do away with the root of the evil." The voices outside grew angrier.

"Did the apothecary have the plague?" Michael whispered.

"No. It was something in his lungs. With plague you have sores that swell up and get black and burst open, and all kinds of other symptoms."

The hammering at the door continued.

"I knew this would happen," Karl sighed. "I'll have to leave the village now. They won't let me stay here. Everyone has been afraid of plague for the last two months."

"That was when my father died," Michael explained. "Lots of people thought he had the plague. Most of our field workers ran away and never came back." "And that's why the Hutterites are there," he almost said, but for once, he curbed the impulse to talk.

The pounding at the door died away.

"What am I going to do now?" Karl asked half to himself. "I don't dare stay here." He put a hand to his forehead and sighed again.

"Come home with me," Michael blurted, then felt an immediate pang. What would Mother say? But Karl looked so happy Michael did not have the heart to withdraw the invitation.

"I guess there's plenty of room in that big castle you live in. I've passed it on my way to the caves."

"What caves?"

"Up in the hills. Most people don't know they are there. I found them once when I was looking for some herbs. Maybe we can go exploring some time." Karl went to the door and listened. "They've gone. We can leave."

Outside, Michael and Karl looked up and down the steep street. No one seemed to be around. Then a shop door not far away banged shut.

"Plague carriers!" a shopkeeper called.

In the apartments above the shops, neighbor called to neighbor. Shutters closed, but not before the terror of the villagers leaped from family to family. Children wailed behind closed doors.

Michael shrank, longing for the safety of home.

"Don't blame the villagers for being afraid," Karl told him. "When I'm a doctor, I'll cure the plague. Dr. von Hohenheim says there's a cure for everything."

"I'd like to be a doctor, too," Michael said.

"Well, you can't just say you're going to be a doctor," Karl explained. "You have to have a calling."

27

"What does that mean?" Michael asked.

"You just have to know, without a shadow of a doubt, that you are supposed to be a doctor."

Michael was silent. He knew he wasn't that sure.

A stocky youth with a walking stick strutted down the street.

"Look, Michael. There's a medical student," Karl whispered. "See his yellow scarf?"

The student waved his walking stick at them. "Allow me to introduce myself, since you two don't look too much like dolts. My name is Oswald Sroll. Why is the village all bolted down? Is it a holy day?"

"No," Karl said. "The villagers are afraid of plague."

"Hmmm. Maybe that's why the doctor came here," Oswald mused.

"Are you studying with Dr. von Hohenheim?" Karl asked.

"I am studying with the great doctor Paracelsus," Oswald corrected Karl, "he who is greater than Celsus, the famous doctor of the first century."

Karl frowned in annoyance. Michael knew his own face was a blank. He had never heard of Celsus.

Oswald explained condescendingly, "Lots of famous men take Latin names -- Frobenius, Oecolampadius, and so on."

Michael still did not understand.

"'Para' is the Latin word meaning 'beyond.'" Oswald's cockiness jarred Michael clear to his toes. "Para-Celsus. Above Celsus. Get it?"

In spite of Oswald's lofty manner, Michael was secretly glad to learn the mystery of Paracelsus' two names.

"I've been trying to catch up with the good doctor for several days now," Oswald sighed. "He's a world traveler, you know. The only reason he's here in Moravia is to find out what the Hutterites know about medicine."

Michael explained that Paracelsus was treating a local nobleman, and Oswald left with a parting remark. "I'd better find him. If Paracelsus didn't have someone to look after him, he wouldn't change his clothes for a month. When he's busy cooking his medicines or writing his books, he sleeps in his clothes, and his sword, too." With a wave of his walking stick, Oswald swaggered away.

Michael and Karl left the closed and shuttered village. On the way to the castle, Karl stopped to catch his breath. "I don't feel good," he admitted. Inside the castle walls, he slumped near the gate. "I'll stay here while you find out from your mother if it's all right for me to stay with you."

Michael hurried to Gudryn's room, delivered the medicine, and waited for the doctor to finish talking to Mother.

Leonard, the old servant, came upstairs. "Madame, the apothecary's boy has fallen all of a heap by the main gate. I prodded him with my foot, but he did not stir."

"Oh, Mother," Michael exclaimed. "That's Karl Gunter. The apothecary died today, and Karl doesn't have any parents, so I -- " Michael gulped. Would his impulsive invitation bring more trouble?

"You what?"

"I invited him to stay here."

Leonard wrung his hands. "What if this illness is catching?"

Michael realized what he had done. True, he had invited Karl out of kindness, but what if Karl had brought the terrible plague with him? It would be Michael's fault.

3

Unpleasant Surprise

On Mother's orders, servants carried Karl to a niche off the kitchen.

"Madame should have said the dungeon," Leonard grumbled.

The dungeon, a twelve-foot deep, circular, stone-lined pit beyond the kitchen, had not been used for years. The servants laid Karl on a straw bed nearby.

Karl raised up on one elbow, his face feverish and his eyes bright. "Find Dr. Hohenheim — Paracelsus," he begged Michael. "He can cure me."

With his new friend and his sister both ill, Michael determined to convince Mother that Paracelsus should be their doctor.

He found Mother downstairs. "I've found the right doctor for Gudryn," he announced.

"The right doctor? What do you mean? Who?"

"Dr. von Hohenheim," Michael said.

"I've never heard that name before. Is he a city doctor?"

"No," Michael answered. "He's a doctor for everybody."

"What did you say his name was?"

"Dr. von Hohenheim." Michael could not hide a smile.

"Why are you smiling?"

"Mother, it's the man called Paracelsus."

Mother frowned.

"He said God is the first physician," Michael rushed on.

Mother tilted her head as if listening to something far away. "God is the first physician," she murmured.

"And the city doctor said Gudryn would never walk again," Michael blurted.

"What!" Mother was horrified.

"Mother, please let Paracelsus see Gudryn. Karl knows him. Paracelsus was in his hometown when the plague was there. People ran away and left the sick people, but Paracelsus helped everyone, rich or poor." Michael did not add that Paracelsus had been run out of town because he had cured so many people they thought he was in league with the devil.

Mother hesitated. "Very well, let him come."

Leonard hurried up to them. "Oh, Madame, it's terrible, terrible! The two dairymaids are deathly ill."

"What with?"

"I suspect the worst."

"You mean --"

"Madame, I mean the plague."

Mother pressed her hands together. "Put the maids in the haying shed."

"No one will touch them," Leonard told her. "I myself am too old and weak."

"Then ask the Hutterites to help you."

Leonard shuddered. "But --"

"But what?" Mother asked sternly.

"The others say the Hutterites are to blame for all this illness."

"Ridiculous," Mother retorted. "They are honest, God-fearing folk."

Leonard took a deep breath. "Madame will forgive me, but --" He looked down at the stone-flagged floor.

"Go on."

"Madame will remember that I warned her about the Hutterites. Everyone says God is punishing us." He clasped his hands. "Won't you send the Hutterites away?"

Mother shook her head. "No, but it may please you to know that I am permitting Dr. von Hohenheim to come here."

At Leonard's blank expression, Mother added, "He's also known as Paracelsus."

Leonard looked so pleased that Michael hoped he would forget about the Hutterites.

Paracelsus himself showed up soon after. "I

understand there is illness here," he told Mother.

Mother shrank from Paracelsus' ragged clothes. Michael glimpsed a soiled leather apron under his cloak.

"Madame, do not shrink from my rags. Do not find fault with me for my rough speech. I am a rough man, born in a rough country. I have been brought up among pine trees, and I may have inherited some knots. That which seems polite to me may appear unpolished to another, and what seems silk in my eyes may seem homespun to you."

"What was it you said about God being the physician?" Mother asked.

"Madame, He is the first. There are many ignorant physicians, but they are the servants of hell, sent by the devil to torment the sick. The true physician is God."

By this time Michael knew the servants had found out Paracelsus was in the castle. Some made several trips upstairs, passing as close as possible to the famous miracle doctor, who stood in the lower hall talking to Mother.

The city doctor stormed out of Gudryn's room and hurried downstairs. "Madame, do I understand you have engaged another physician without consulting me?"

"This is Dr. von Hohenheim."

"Ah," the city doctor responded in an icy tone, "the medical Luther."

Paracelsus bristled. "Why do you call me 'the

medical Luther'? You do not intend to honor me by giving me that name, because you despise Luther."

"I have read your 'Great Surgery Book.' Like Luther, you write in German, not Latin. Like him, you are breaking with all past traditions. I suppose you are here to work one of your so-called miracles," the city doctor sneered.

"God does not perform miracles without man," Paracelsus answered. "He acts through m-m-man."

The city doctor bowed in mockery. "Spoken like the great and illustrious Theophrastus Bombastus von Hohenheim himself. Too bad you don't have a doctor's degree."

"I took my degree in Ferrara," Paracelsus said.

"Ah, Italy." A note of respect deepened the city doctor's voice. "How do you explain about Basel, where you didn't present your diploma before the faculty of the university?"

"A doctor is known by his works," Paracelsus retorted. "If you must have proof of my degree, read the second part of my 'Great Surgery Book.' In the third treatise, I have given the course of studies I took for my doctor's degree. But I really learned to be a doctor by questioning bath attendants, herbwomen, gypsies, monks, and peasants. I have traveled in Sweden, Germany, Poland, Austria, Hungary, Italy, Sicily --"

"Spare me, spare me," the court doctor said angrily. "How would you have time enough in one lifetime to do all that? Perhaps that is why he dresses in rags," he muttered and turned to Mother. "Madame, are you going to let this gypsy doctor, this heathen, this sorcerer, stay here? This man is an imposter. He has been run out of every town he lived in. He tries to tell city officials how to keep their citizens healthy, against all known laws of medicine. Not only is he a quack, he tries to make gold out of base metals."

At this attack Paracelsus clenched his fists. "I am no gold cook, no matter what stories ignorant people tell. I am a Christian and walk in the light of Christ. I will not be called sorcerer, or heathen, or gypsy, but profess myself a Christian. Let false Christians sweat with their own sour dough."

The two doctors glared at each other.

A maidservant ran out of Gudryn's room. "Oh, Madame, the child has thrown herself out of bed."

"Please help her, Dr. von Hohenheim," Mother pleaded.

Everyone crowded into the sickroom.

"Take her pulse," Paracelsus ordered, after placing Gudryn on the bed. The city doctor's assistant picked up Gudryn's limp wrist.

"All that has been done," the city doctor snapped. In an aside he said to his assistant, "Now you have the opportunity to watch a quack doctor at work." After Paracelsus had examined Gudryn, the city doctor sneered, "Why don't you diagnose the ailment and give a prescription?"

"I do not know at once what ails the girl," Paracelsus told him. "I need time to find out. You city doctors diagnose immediately. That is foolish. A physician must be thoroughly familiar with an illness before he can know what medicine to use. Learned fools only make their patients worse."

The city doctor's cheeks puffed with anger, but Michael could see that he had no intention of leaving the castle. His fee, Michael knew, would be even higher now that Paracelsus had been called in.

Mother asked in a whisper, "Is it true that she is paralyzed?"

Paracelsus scowled at the city doctor before replying. "Let no doctor say a sickness is incurable. He who says so denies God our Creator. There is no disease so great that He has not provided its cure. In medicine we should never lose heart and never despair. For each ill there is a remedy that combats it. There is no disease that is inevitably mortal. All diseases can be cured, without exception." He bowed to Mother. "And now, Madame, if you would be so kind as to show me where I may have a little fire, I will make the medicine that will help your daughter."

The city doctor snorted. "You and your talk of God! Why not let Him supply the medicine?"

"God did not choose to give us the medicines already prepared. He wants us to cook them ourselves," Paracelsus said.

"Michael," Mother directed, "show Dr. von Hohenheim to the back kitchen where he may have a fire."

Michael took Paracelsus down a tiny circular staircase at the end of the hall and showed him a place near the kitchen where he could make a fire. Paracelsus lost no time ordering the kitchen servants to build a hot fire. Michael whispered to Karl that Paracelsus was in the castle but would first help Gudryn. "Then he'll help you and the others."

Paracelsus brought in his saddlebags, refusing offers of help. He unbuckled his sword, and after a glance at the servants, as if trying to decide whether anyone would steal it, he placed the sword near the fire. The action puzzled Michael. As a doctor, Paracelsus was surely too busy to use a sword. Why was he so careful with it? Perhaps it was a gift from a grateful patient. The sword was entirely out of keeping with the rags Paracelsus wore.

Michael watched Paracelsus mix several strong-smelling liquids. Using a long-handled pan, Paracelsus knelt before the fire and turned the pan this way and that until the liquid seethed. Some splashed on his leather apron.

Paracelsus believed God provided a cure for every disease. Man must find it.

From time to time, servants peeked at the famous doctor making medicine. Michael overheard them talking among themselves.

"They say he makes gold," one said loud enough to be heard by Paracelsus.

"The object of chemistry is not to make gold but to prepare healing drugs," he said, as if addressing a group of medical students.

Even the city doctor and his assistant came to stare at the medicine-making.

"Do you smell that concoction?" The assistant held his nose between forefinger and thumb. "It smells like sulfur."

"It smells like the devil, then," the city doctor chuckled. "People say he's sold his soul like Dr. Faustus. May the devil take him, too."

When Paracelsus finished the medicine, only a few drops remained. Michael was amazed. All that work for such a little dab? Why did it take so much work?

"Does grain grow into loaves of bread?" Paracelsus asked him.

Michael laughed. "Of course not. You have to harvest the grain, make it into flour, mix dough, and then bake it."

"If you want grape juice, do the grapes jump off the vine and come running to you?"

"No. You have to pick them and squeeze the juice out."

"Did God make the grain and the grapes?"

"Of course."

Paracelsus pounded a handful of dried herbs with an iron pestle. "Medicines," he panted between strokes, "are created by God, but not in their finished state. That is true of everything He has given us. The art of medicine lies in separating the useful from the useless."

"Miracle cures," everyone said a few days later. Gudryn, able to walk after her second fall from bed, was cured of her lung congestion by Paracelsus' treatment. Karl and the sick servants recovered when they took the medicine Paracelsus made for each one.

"Impostor!" the city doctor exclaimed. He demanded a large fee and left with his assistant. "I'll show up this doctor for the quack he is."

The threat bothered Michael, but with Karl and Gudryn well, there was too much for all three to do around the castle to waste time worrying about the city doctor's threat.

First, Michael showed Karl and Gudryn where the Hutterites had traced the outlines of their community dining hall and other buildings for the Bruderhof. Piles of timber from the hills lay in neat piles.

"Did you know our whole estate could be confiscated by the king?" Gudryn demanded one day. "I heard the servants talking about it."

"If they don't tell the king's men, no one will know," Michael said, trying to hide his own secret worry.

Next, the villagers found out that the miracle

doctor was at the castle. They flocked to the castle and begged him to cure their sick. Soon Paracelsus was administering to the entire neighborhood.

"Did you know that Paracelsus always tells his patients about God's Word?" Karl asked one day.

"That's because patients have to have faith, or they won't get well," Gudryn said. "He asked me how strong my faith was, and of course I said it was strong enough to cure me -- if Paracelsus would help. He nodded and said I was already recovering. And it was true."

"Maybe that's why he wants to study with the Hutterite doctors," Karl said. He had already talked to some of the Hutterite builders. "They call some of their doctors medical missioners. They not only heal people but they tell about God."

One day a horseman came to the castle with a tiny pouch of coins to pay Paracelsus for curing his master, the count.

Michael, Karl, and Gudryn watched Paracelsus accept the pouch with a smile. "Thank the count for me. The sixty florins will come in handy."

The messenger coughed and hurried away.

Paracelsus opened the pouch. "Six florins -- not the sixty that the count promised." He burst into an ironic laugh, and with a mock flourish, bowed toward the retreating horseman. "I expect thanks from no one." He went back to his niche by the kitchen to make more medicine.

A villager came to pay Paracelsus. "He saved my whole family, cured them one by one," he told Michael, Karl, and Gudryn. "He brought a Bible and read out of it, and then left the Bible with us. Now I know more about God than I ever learned in all my life before."

Michael explained that Paracelsus was making medicine for other patients.

"Then give him this herb. It's all the payment I can make. It took me many days to find it up in the hills. He told me if I found it, that would more than pay his fee."

Other villagers paid what they could, grateful for what Paracelsus had done. Michael, Karl, and Gudryn took turns in taking the fees to Paracelsus.

One day when Michael was alone at the gate, Oswald, the medical student, appeared, cocky as ever. He planted his two fists on his hips and surveyed the castle and courtyard. "So this is where Paracelsus lives. Too bad he has to leave."

The very thought made Michael feel sick to his stomach. "He's not leaving."

"Oh, yes, he is. I've been staying at the inn, and I've heard people talking. The village authorities are up in arms. It's the same story as before. Paracelsus cures so many illnesses people are afraid of his power." Oswald waved an airy good-bye. "Wait and see. They're going to run Paracelsus out of the district."

All of Michael's fears jumbled together -- the Hutterites being on the estate against the law, Paracelsus, and the authorities. "I must warn him," Michael thought. He started toward the castle. A sudden dizziness hit him. Perspiration broke out on his hands and forehead. He sank down, astonished that his legs would not hold him up. "I'm sick," he told himself, and knew he was not going to be able to warn anyone.

4
Secret Medicine

Michael woke with a throbbing head. Where were all the loud voices coming from? He stirred, tried to lift his head and see beyond the curtains of his bed, but fell back with a groan. At once the curtains parted. Karl's face appeared framed in the opening.

"You're awake. I'll tell your mother."

Michael heard the bustle of feet, murmurs of servants. Someone dabbed at his forehead with a wrung-out wet cloth.

"Madame, is he all right?" The frightened voice of a maidservant reached Michael as if through a hollow tube. He tried to say, "Of course I'm all right," but his lips refused to open. His tongue stuck to the roof of his mouth. He was astonished that he could not command himself to speak. All that came was another groan.

"Oh, Madame, is he dying?"

"No, of course not," Mother said, but she sounded worried.

"Madame, Paracelsus has a medicine that will cure anything," the servant said. "It's a secret medicine. He keeps it in the pommel of his sword. The cook saw him unscrew the top of his sword and take some out when your daughter was so ill."

"I'm sure the doctor will find the right medicine," Mother said.

Servants scurried in and out. At each step, Michael's head throbbed more.

"He's feverish. Sponge his face."

The damp cloth on his forehead felt good. Michael drifted in and out of sleep. Several voices sounded together. Michael was puzzled. Was Oswald, the know-it-all, in the room? How did he get in?

Now Paracelsus seemed to be giving a lecture. Then Michael remembered. Karl was going to be a doctor. What better teacher could he have than Paracelsus? What better classroom than Michael's own sickbed?

"Note how nature struggles against sickness with all her power," Paracelsus said. "We must follow the disease like a cow following the grass in the meadow. Remember, there is always a remedy, an herb for one disease, a root for another; a water for one, a stone for another; a mineral for one, a poison for another."

"Are you going to give him a poison?" Michael heard Oswald ask.

"What has God created that He did not bless with some great gift for the benefit of man?" Paracelsus asked in turn. "Is not a mystery of nature concealed even in poison? I am not frightened because one part of a remedy is poisonous. Each thing must be used for its proper purpose. It depends only upon the dose whether a poison acts as a poison or not. In small doses, it may be an antidote."

Michael lay with his eyes closed. The voices in the room sounded far away. Paracelsus asked Oswald to watch the fire downstairs.

"Why do you have to cook your medicines?" he grumbled. "It takes so long."

"We must learn all things with labor and difficulty," Paracelsus told him. "It is not God's design that remedies should exist for us but that we should boil them ourselves."

"They say you boil gold in your furnaces," Oswald blurted.

Paracelsus burst into a scornful laugh. "Ah, are you one of those gold-cooks? They have a golden mountain in their heads before they put their hands into the charcoal."

"But I heard how you cured a farmer's wife in Ambras with a wonder drug, and when you came that way again, she was so grateful you took a kitchen fork, smeared it with yellow ointment, and it turned into solid gold. Another time, your helper Franz brought you a pound of mercury. You put it over a fire, and after a while, you lifted it out and it was a solid gold lump."

Paracelsus laughed so hard, Michael realized the doctor had just been playing a joke.

Later, when Karl and Oswald were alone with Michael, Oswald showed off in his usual overbearing way. "Did you know that doctors pledge themselves never to use the knife?"

"Why not?"

"They're not supposed to risk dirtying their hands by touching intestines, like butchers. That's a barber-surgeon's duty. Doctors don't apply dressings nor perform operations," Oswald said.

"Maybe they don't now, but they will in the future. You'd better read Paracelsus' Great Surgery book." Karl sounded irritated.

"Learned doctors don't even see the patient," Oswald went on.

"How do they know what to prescribe?"

"You've heard of Albrecht Dürer, the painter, I suppose. He sent a sketch to the doctor marked, 'This is the place I hurt.'"

Karl grunted with either amusement or scorn. Michael wasn't sure. Oswald's chatter annoyed him, yet it was interesting. But if Oswald thought Paracelsus was a great doctor, why did he always argue so much?

Paracelsus was busy from daylight to far into the night. He treated patients from the village, cooked medicines for them, and wrote up his medical notes. One evening at Michael's bedside, Paracelsus put his hands to his face and toppled onto the bed, sound asleep.

A little later, Michael heard a rustle. The door opened. Oswald, holding a small torch, cocked his head as if listening and crept toward the bed.

Every muscle in Michael's body tensed. "What's he up to?" he thought, more baffled than afraid.

Oswald tiptoed to Paracelsus, put the torch in a holder by the bed, and reached for the knob on Paracelsus' sword. The doctor jerked upright. "Stop! What are you doing?" He grabbed Oswald at the back of his neck like a kitten and shook him.

"The secret medicine," Oswald babbled. "I wanted just a pinch. There's an old man ill here in the castle. The servants say you have a magic medicine that cures people instantly."

"That medicine is the most powerful in the world." At every word Paracelsus gave Oswald another shake. "God permitted me to discover it, but it is never, never, to be used by anyone other than a physician."

Michael half-heard the words. Old man. There was only one in the castle. "Who is sick?" he asked Oswald.

"They call him Leonard."

The name rang in Michael's ears like a death knell. With so much sickness around, would Leonard have strength enough to recover? He started up out of bed.

"Here! Where are you going?" Paracelsus asked.

"I want to see how Leonard is."

"You stay here. I'll attend to him." Paracelsus left the room.

Not long afterward, Paracelsus reported Leonard's death. Michael turned his face to the wall. "Couldn't you have saved him with your secret medicine?"

"There is no drug, no herb that will keep death away," Paracelsus explained. "No doctor can help when the end has come."

Later, after a dose of Paracelsus' medicine, Michael complained, "I feel on fire."

"Good."

Michael bristled. "How can it be good?"

"The remedy should operate in the body like a fire. Its effect should be as violent as fire on a pile of wood."

"But the dose was so small."

"A spark can set a forest on fire, a little spark that has no weight at all," Paracelsus said.

Michael thought about the mystery of healing. Even when he was well, he could not forget the death of Leonard, the old servant. "Why does God let people die?" he asked.

"Death or decay is the beginning of all birth," was Paracelsus' prompt reply.

"What?" Michael exclaimed.

"Only when food decays in the stomach and is made into a pulp can it be used in the body. Decay causes rot so that a noble fruit may be born.

A seed must rot away if it is to bear fruit."

Michael puzzled over this remark for days. He wondered about illness and health, life and death. He questioned Paracelsus again.

" 'That which is born of the flesh, and that which is born of the Spirit is spirit.' Death is day's work ended and God's harvesttime. Man's power over us ends at death and only God deals with us then, and God is love."

Michael had never heard anyone in all his life talk in such a way, but he began to catch a faint glimpse of what Paracelsus meant. The more Michael thought about it, the more he felt he should become a doctor, too, like Karl, who seemed to have no trouble understanding Paracelsus' ideas. But Paracelsus himself was now in trouble.

The news of Leonard's death had spread. Paracelsus' enemies rejoiced. Here was the excuse they had been looking for. The doctor's many remarkable cures meant nothing. A man had died, and Paracelsus was to blame.

The city doctor swept into the castle with two colleagues and a group of city officials. They strode up and down in the entrance hall waiting for Paracelsus to return from a visit to a patient.

"Isn't there any way we can warn Paracelsus?" Gudryn whispered to Michael and Karl.

"It wouldn't do any good," Karl said. "He would have to face them sometime." He hit his fist into his open palm. "It isn't fair."

Mother came in with a worried frown and stood with Michael, Karl, and Gudryn.

The city doctor thumped his cane on the floor. He called across to Mother. "Madame, you wanted this Paracelsus, this so-called doctor in his filthy rags. You got him. Now you see that he cannot do one thing of which he boasts. Your old, faithful servant is dead. And why? Because this quack said to wait, as he always does. Wait for what? The sun to sink in the west and cover his ignorance in the merciful cloak of darkness? Wait so that after filling his belly with fine food, he can slip out with some of the master's fine clothes to parade in the next town, where he'll scurry under cover of darkness? Madame, admit it. You have been completely taken in by this impostor. All his so-called miracle cures will not bring back the dead to life."

Mother listened without a word. Michael knew she dreaded to have the officials learn of the Hutterites on the estate. He could read on her face the hope that no mention of the forbidden group would be made.

The men began to talk about Paracelsus.

"Yes, yes, he's an imposter," one said. "In 1534 he applied to practice medicine in Innsbruck and the petition was denied. The city council said that a man in rags was not a doctor."

"I have heard of him," another said. "He's a braggart, always on edge, always criticizing a city's health laws, trying to push his own ideas.

He makes a few cures that the lowest barber-surgeon could accomplish, quarrels with the people who find out he's a fraud, and finally runs away."

A third chimed in. "He has been that way all his life. Remember the St. John's Day uprising in 1527? It was more than the students' usual Midsummer Night's antics. Paracelsus and his students threw Avicenna's book on the fire."

The others spluttered their indignation. "Why, Avicenna is the very father of medicine," the city doctor said.

The other speaker agreed. "But our Paracelsus — he who is above Celsus," he added in scorn, "claimed when he burned Avicenna's book that the realm of medicine had been purged and a new age of medicine had begun."

"How about the Basel episode?" someone asked.

The city doctor eagerly replied. "The university was suspicious from the first. He never called on the faculty as was customary. The university wouldn't let him lecture on the campus."

"Where did he teach, then?"

"He hired an off-campus hall."

"Who came?"

"Well," the city doctor grudgingly admitted, "he had thirty graduate students."

There were whistles of astonishment. The questions continued.

"What did he teach?"

53

"Pathology, therapeutics, pharmacology, diagnostics, purgation, injuries, disorders requiring surgery. You name it, he taught it," the city doctor said. "Not only that, but he spoke German in his surgical lectures."

"Unheard of," the others murmured.

"That's because he doesn't know enough Latin, of course," the city doctor added.

One man spoke up. "In all fairness, I happen to know that Paracelsus bought citizenship in Strasbourg in 1526. The records state that he was received as a doctor of both medicines into the Guild of the Alfalfa, which admits doctors, millers, and grain merchants. As you perhaps know, Strasbourg is the only place where surgeons have equal rights with physicians."

An official scratched his head. "I am puzzled about one thing. Does he have his doctor's degree or doesn't he?"

"He has none," the city doctor snapped. "He can show nothing."

A shout of anger stopped him. Paracelsus, pale and shaking, stood at the doorway, looking from one to another. Michael watched with a sinking feeling. He knew that Paracelsus was pouring all his energies into making medicines, curing people, and writing up his case histories for other doctors to follow. Now he was being accused of not having the right to do it.

"I hope he doesn't lose his temper," Karl whispered. "That's what happened before. He says things on impulse, and then it's too late."

Michael suddenly realized why Mother had chided him for being impulsive. It could really be dangerous.

Paracelsus' eyes sparkled with rage. "What is the use of name, title, and school unless doctors have the knowledge? Who deserves the doctor's ring and cloak but those who deserve them by their skill? If disease puts us to the test, all our splendid clothes, title, ring, and name will be as much help as a horse's tail."

Karl whispered to Michael, "But he is a doctor. He took his degree at Ferrara. Why doesn't he defend himself?"

Paracelsus had barely started. "The act of healing makes the physician, not emperor nor pope, faculty or university. But what do I see everywhere?" He cast a contemptuous glance at the city doctor and his colleagues. "I see men who see to their own profit, and who take delight in letting me starve and perish. I see men who lie about me to the patients, who receive patients behind my back, without my knowledge, who t-t-treat them for half the money saying that they know my art, that they have watched me do it. Shall this make me sweet as a lamb? Even a peaceful turtledove would be enraged by these sordid b-b-beasts."

"You have entered the temple of knowledge by a back door," someone ventured.

"So you complain that I have not entered the

temple of knowledge through the right door. But which one is the right one -- Galen, Avicenna, or nature? I have entered the door of nature. God has given His power to the herbs, put it in stones, concealed it in seeds. He provides the healing means in nature and He directs their discovery and use. God made me a doctor. Not only I but every man who calls himself a doctor should always have God before his eyes."

"The Luther of medicine," someone muttered.

The remark touched off more fury in Paracelsus. "Let Luther justify his own affairs and I will account for mine. Who are Luther's foes? Those who hate me. And what you wish to him, you wish to me -- to the f-f-fire with us both." In his rage, Paracelsus stuttered more than ever. His listeners backed away from the fiery torrent of words.

"You have no right to practice medicine," the city doctor maintained.

"Have I not cured eighteen princes after other doctors had given them up? I have healed forty different diseases. You, who defend your kingdom with belly-crawling and flattery, let me tell you this: every little hair on my neck knows more than you and all your scribes. My shoe-buckles are more learned than your Galen and Avicenna."

A messenger entered the castle, looked at the group of angry men, and hesitated. "I have a message for the great doctor Paracelsus."

Paracelsus looked at him wearily. "What kind of message?"

"A summons."

A summons. Michael knew only one meaning for that word. A summons meant imprisonment for wrongdoing.

All the fire and anger in Paracelsus left him. He stood with shoulders sagging, his hand on the pommel of his sword. But the secret medicine he carried there would not help him now.

5
Buried Treasure

For a moment there was not a sound in the entrance hall from the angry men who had been denouncing Paracelsus. Michael tensed. What would happen next?

The messenger stared at Paracelsus' downcast head. "There is nothing to be alarmed about, sir. It is true I was not the messenger who brought the first summons to you when you were visiting Dr. Johann von Brandt at Eferdingen a short time ago, but this summons is an honor. It is from Johann von der Leipnik, the Chief Hereditary Marshall of Bohemia. He begs you to come to Kromau and cure him of his lingering illness. He sends you this purse." The messenger held out a pouch heavy with coins.

Paracelsus waved off the money. "I cannot

accept money for something I have not done. For all I know, the Marshal may be dead already."

The messenger pulled out a letter. "Here is a report from the attending physician." He waited until Paracelsus read it. "The Marshal has a great deal of influence. I am sure he will see to it that no difficulties stand in the way of your coming."

At these words, the city doctor and the other men hurried away.

"They don't dare do anything now," Michael exulted. He and Mother persuaded Paracelsus to buy suitable clothes for the journey. Paracelsus left, equipped with a new horse, saddle, riding gear, coat, mantle, hat, boots, and spurs. He carefully packed his manuscripts in two saddlebags, one on each side of the horse.

"Now you look important," Gudryn said, "the way a doctor should."

Paracelsus laughed. "The physician must not think himself too important, for over him there is a master -- time -- which plays with him as the cat with the mouse."

The whole household gathered around the gate to bid Paracelsus good-bye. Oswald drifted up to the group.

"Are you going with him?" Gudryn asked.

"I have other things to attend to," he told her.

"But I thought you were his disciple."

Oswald replied with a shrug.

Michael puzzled over Oswald's remark about having other things to attend to. The secretive Oswald had wandered between castle and village for some time, sometimes helping Paracelsus, sometimes off on his own.

"What do you think he's up to?" Michael whispered to Karl. To his surprise, Karl ran up to Paracelsus.

"May I go with you?" Karl asked. "I want to be a doctor."

Paracelsus turned from tightening a strap on a saddlebag and smiled. "Do not be like so many who do not want to learn first things first. Everyone wants to fly before he has grown wings. Stay here and learn from the Hutterites."

Karl nodded.

"Perhaps later, who knows? We may meet again." Paracelsus started off on his journey to Kromau.

After Paracelsus' departure, Michael and Karl watched the Hutterites at work. A horseman rode up and watched, too.

"Who's that?" Karl asked.

"No one I've ever seen." Michael tried to shake off an uneasy feeling.

"Maybe he's a Hutterite overseer."

"He couldn't be," Michael said. "He's not dressed like a Hutterite." The uneasy feeling persisted. Could the horseman be a spy?

The Hutterites emptied sackloads of soil over the fields.

"Why are they doing that?" Karl asked.

"They must still be digging foundations, I suppose." But that seemed odd. The various buildings of the Bruderhof looked almost ready for the roofs.

Gudryn came running across the field to Michael and Karl. "Come quick," she gasped.

"What's the matter?" Michael asked.

"Follow me, and you'll see." She led the way to the kitchen, but did not stop there. Michael guessed where she was going.

"Gudryn, you mean there's a prisoner?"

"Yes, and you'll never guess who."

Michael and Karl peered into the deep, stone-lined pit. Oswald sat against the wall, his knees to his chin, and his tousled head buried in his hands.

"Oswald! What happened?" Michael called.

Oswald looked up. "The servants put me here."

"But why?"

"Something about my being a spy and giving away the secret."

"What secret?" Michael asked.

"About the Hutterites, I suppose."

Michael remembered the horseman. Was there any connection? Still, even if Oswald and his know-it-all ways made him a nuisance, he could not stay in the dungeon. Michael found a knotted rope and wound it around a chopping block. Oswald climbed up with some difficulty. With a grunt of thanks, he left the castle.

The next morning, Oswald came back. "You probably think I gave away the secret about the Hutterites. Well, I didn't. But I'm telling you now that the royal provost and his men are on the way to the castle. You'd better warn the Hutterites to hide."

It took Michael a moment to digest what Oswald was saying.

"Go and look for yourselves," Oswald told Michael and Karl.

They ran to the gate and looked out. A group of horsemen were coming toward the castle.

"Come on, Karl. We'll tell the Hutterites."

When Michael and Karl reached the half-finished Bruderhof, they found the place deserted. Not a Hutterite could be seen.

"Maybe they are in some of the outbuildings," Michael said. He and Karl went to every shed on the estate. All were empty.

Michael looked around in bewilderment. "Where are they? Where could they have gone?"

"To the hills," Karl answered. "The caves. Do you remember my telling you about the caves up there?"

Shouts at the gate interrupted them.

"In the king's name, open the gates," a man demanded from outside.

When the gates were opened, mounted soldiers swarmed in.

"Bring out your household," the royal provost ordered Mother.

When everyone lined up, the royal provost strode back and forth between the line of horsemen and the family.

"Madame," he announced, "you have allowed Hutterites to build a Bruderhof on your estate. This is against the law, as you well know. Show us the place."

Mother motioned to Michael and Karl to show the Bruderhof to the king's men.

The deserted, half-built buildings enraged the provost. He stormed, "Where are the heretics?"

"No one knows. They just disappeared," Michael told him.

"Disappeared? Overnight? Who told them we were coming?"

"I don't know, sir."

The royal provost glared at Michael and Karl. He looked at the deserted buildings again, and with a sly grin returned to Mother.

"King Ferdinand needs money to fight the Turks. Everyone knows Hutterites are rich, because they hoard their money. They've probably buried some right on your estate." The royal provost cleared his throat. "If you will persuade these heretics to pay a tax of one thousand florins, nothing will be said about their staying here. Otherwise --"

"Otherwise, what?" Mother asked.

"We will burn the Bruderhof to the ground."

Mother paled. "But we don't know where they went."

63

"That's not my concern. You have twenty-four hours to raise the money." He turned to the soldiers. "We'll camp here tonight. Until then, at ease."

"They're all coming up the Inn River to Moravia," Michael heard a soldier say. "They call it the promised land."

"They have Bruderhofs all over the country," another added. "How can we hope to destroy them all?"

The men unloaded their equipment and stabled their horses. In a little while they started mock battles and games of skill.

Mother called Michael and Karl. "Do you have any idea where the Hutterites have gone?"

When she learned of the caves she sighed in relief. "Of course! That's the only possible place. Go find them and tell them what has happened."

Michael and Karl started off. Gudryn caught up with them.

"I want to go, too."

"Girls can't climb mountains," Michael said.

"I'm not a weakling," Gudryn retorted with spirit. "I'm strong for my age. I can outrun either of you." Gudryn picked up her skirts, ready to run.

"Well, come on, then," Michael said. "But you've got to keep up with us."

Near the Bruderhof they picked their way single file over fresh dirt. Michael watched every step.

"Stop!" Gudryn called in a loud whisper. "Someone's digging by that tree over there."

Michael glanced up. "It's Oswald."

Oswald had taken off his outer cloak. With frantic haste he was shoveling dirt near the foot of the tree.

"What are you doing, Oswald?" Michael asked.

With a yelp of surprise, Oswald whirled around. "If you must know," he panted, "I'm looking for buried gold."

"What gold?"

"Didn't you hear the provost say that Hutterites bury their money? Why should the king get it? He'd just use it to carry on wars. I'll take it myself, and no one can stop me."

"But that's stealing," Gudryn said.

Oswald shrugged. "The Hutterites have abandoned this place." He folded his arms as if waiting to be left alone.

There was no time to argue. Michael, Karl, and Gudryn left the field and started for the hills. Karl took the lead.

"Do you think anyone will follow us?" Gudryn asked, with quick glances over her shoulder.

"Anyone who doesn't know the way would soon be lost," Karl said. "See how thick the shrubs are."

They pushed by trees and clumps of bushes almost straight uphill. Michael glimpsed clefts in the rocks high above. Karl led the way up the narrow forest trail. Sometimes big boulders blocked the way and the trail disappeared.

"You'd think the Hutterites put these stones here on purpose," Gudryn complained.

"I think I know the secret of all that dirt they put on the fields," Karl said.

"What is it?" Michael and Gudryn chorused.

"I don't want to say so yet, but I'll tell you the minute I see the signs."

At one place a huge rock blocked the way. There was no way up or down or around. Shrubs grew at each side. "The trail ends here," Michael said in disappointment.

"We'll never find the Hutterites," Gudryn sighed.

"No, here's a cleft," Karl called. At one side of the boulder he pointed out an opening hardly big enough for a person to squeeze through. "Exactly what I thought," he exulted. "There's a cave here."

The cave, like a grotto, opened unexpectedly back of the boulder. A moss-covered tree had toppled over the entrance. Karl held the heavy branches back, and Michael and Gudryn stepped inside. The cave was hardly big enough to stand up in, but was wide. The walls oozed moisture.

Gudryn, Karl, and Michael at a cave entrance trying to find and warn the Hutterites of danger of arrest.

Michael examined the floor of the cave. "Look at all the footprints. They're in here someplace."

"Let's call them," Gudryn suggested.

"Hello," they called. An echo mocked them.

"How far back does the cave go?" Michael felt along the wall. "Here's a cave branching off," he exclaimed after a few moments.

"Just what I thought," Karl said. "This isn't a cave. It's a tunnel. That's what those sacks were. They would dig out this tunnel and bring the dirt back and put it on the fields all the time they were building the Bruderhof. No wonder it went so slowly."

Michael made another discovery. Two tunnels branched off at sharp angles.

Karl puzzled over the reason. "I don't think anyone is here, but how did they get out? The footprints all go in and none come back."

"Do you think the Hutterites are all huddled up in one of these tunnels?" Gudryn asked.

"Let's find out," Michael said. "We'll have to, if we expect to catch up with them." He shivered a little at the thought of plunging into one of the dark, narrow tunnels, but he wasn't going to let Gudryn know he was afraid.

"We'll have to explore each tunnel," Karl said. "You and Gudryn take one and I'll take the other."

To Michael's surprise, the tunnel he and Gudryn explored led right back into the antechamber through a third opening which they had not noticed before.

They waited for Karl. He did not come back. They called and called. The only answer was silence after the hollow echo of their own voices. Michael chided himself. He should not have let Karl go alone. They should have all stayed together.

A shuffling sound over the cave entrance startled Michael. Stones trickled from overhead and fell with loud plops. Gudryn grabbed Michael's arm in panic. "Someone has followed us. What shall we do?"

Michael's thoughts whirled. Had the king's men followed them to the cave, then realized the Hutterites had hidden there? The stones continued to drop. It would take only a few big boulders to seal the mouth of the cave forever.

6
A Bitter Pill

Someone was thrashing through the underbrush above the cave. The sounds came closer and closer.

"Is it an animal?" Gudryn's question ended in a gasp of fear.

Before Michael could answer, he heard his name called.

"That's Karl! How did he get up there?" Michael seized Gudryn by the hand and they both ran outside.

Karl half-scrambled, half-slid down the steep rock and landed at their feet. His clothes were torn, his hair matted, and two scratches on his face oozed blood. "I found them! They're camped in the woods," he panted.

"How did they get out of the cave?" Michael asked.

"Through my tunnel." Karl brushed loose twigs off his clothes. "They didn't see me. We've got to tell them what the royal provost said. Come on." He led the way through the cave.

After an unexpected sharp turn, Michael found himself outside. He blinked at the sudden daylight.

"The Hutterites are just ahead," Karl whispered.

A group of Hutterites sat on stones or stumps in a jagged semicircle. A leader stood before them and talked in earnest tones.

"How can we keep from scaring them?" Michael whispered. "If they think someone is after them, they'll run."

"Let me call them," Gudryn suggested. "They won't be afraid of a girl." She cupped her hands over her mouth. "Hello, hello."

The Hutterites jumped up. Michael ran to them. "It's all right. No one else knows where you are." He told them of the royal provost's threat to burn the Bruderhof, and also his offer to accept a fine.

At the mention of the thousand florins, the Hutterites shook their heads. "We do not have that much money," they said. "We cannot go back."

"But what about the Bruderhof?" Gudryn asked. "All that work --"

"It is in God's hands," was the answer.

"Where will you go?"

"To Kromau."

"Kromau?" Michael, Karl, and Gudryn chorused.

"Paracelsus is going there, too."

The leader of the Hutterites nodded. "He will visit our Bruderhof there. Johann von Lipa, the Lord of Kromau and Shäkovitz, has ignored orders to expel our brethren. We shall be safe on his estate."

"What about Steinabrunn?" a Hutterite asked. "There's a Bruderhof near the village. I knew some of the brethren there -- Mathes Legeder, Gutenhenn Hans, Michel Blauer, Michel Kramer."

"We cannot discuss this any longer. We shall put ourselves into God's hands. He will direct us." The others agreed and with a prayer started their journey.

Gudryn stared after them. "How peaceful they are. They don't seem to mind leaving everything behind."

"They mind, all right," Michael assured her. "But they have a living trust in God." He was astonished at his own words. He had never before thought this clearly about the faith of people who defied the laws of a king in order to follow the laws of God.

Karl blew on the tiny flame of a makeshift torch a Hutterite had lit for him. "That's true," he told Michael.

"But it doesn't help us," Gudryn sighed. "We've got to go back and tell Mother. And then -- "

Michael knew what she meant. The Bruderhof

on their estate would be burned.

"Come on," Karl urged. "Let's go back through the cave. I want to see how they planned it."

Michael and Gudryn followed Karl. By the light of the torch they discovered how the passage kept changing direction. At one point a pit seemed to mark the end, but the tunnel continued on a higher level reached by a special passage. Karl pointed out niches. "For the watchmen and their lamps," he said.

Michael and Gudryn showed Karl the false tunnel near the entrance.

"I'm glad the Hutterites are going to be safe at Kromau," Gudryn said. "How terrible to be hunted all the time and never know where you were going to sleep from one night to the next."

"It took a lot of work to make this hiding place," Karl said. "They must have known other Hutterites might have to use it."

"We won't tell the royal provost where the cave is, then."

Rough voices sounded through the trees on the slope outside the cave.

"The soldiers! They're coming after us," Gudryn gasped.

Karl stamped out the torch light. "I don't think they'll find us. We didn't beat down a trail when we came up the hill. You can see for yourself that shrubs grow high and hide the mouth of the cave."

The men outside shouted to each other on their

way through the trees. Michael pressed back into a tunnel with Karl and Gudryn. A soldier found the cave entrance and bellowed the news to his companions.

"Come on out, you Hutterite heretics. We know you are there. Come out in the king's name."

"Don't answer," Karl hissed. "The longer we delay them, the more chance the Hutterites have to get away."

Michael heard the men arguing outside.

"They're in there, all right. How shall we get them out?"

"Seal the cave," one soldier suggested.

"What! And have the people make martyrs of them? No, that would never do. Besides, King Ferdinand wants to reconvert them. He wants the priests to talk them out of their false beliefs."

"Why don't we smoke them out?" another soldier suggested.

Michael heard the rustle of twigs and branches being placed near the entrance.

"They don't know we can escape through the back way," Gudryn said with a nervous giggle.

"We mustn't let them know about the back way," Karl said. "Let them think this is just a cave."

"Hurry! Before they light the fire," Michael answered.

The three left the cave one by one. A group of soldiers stared at them.

"Look! They are nothing but children," a soldier said in a disgusted voice.

"Where are the Hutterites?" another soldier thundered.

"We don't know." Michael knew that was the truth.

Karl and Gudryn said they did not know, either.

"Perhaps a little taste of prison life might help them to remember. Isn't there a dungeon in the castle?"

Were the soldiers really serious about imprisoning them? One glance at their grim faces convinced Michael. He thought of the stone pit at the castle. No one could get out of it without help. Panic swept over him in waves. Why had Mother let the Hutterites come to the estate in the first place? Then Michael felt ashamed. The Hutterites lived in fear of imprisonment or worse all the time. Their only hope was God. If they could believe, he could, too. At that moment, Michael sensed a strange calm.

The soldiers herded Michael, Karl, and Gudryn ahead of them down the wooded hill.

"Are you afraid?" Gudryn murmured.

"Not really," Michael answered and knew it was true.

At the castle, the soldiers brought Michael, Karl, and Gudryn before the royal provost, who was using the gatekeeper's niche as his command post.

"Sir, these children knew where the Hutterites

went, but they won't tell."

The royal provost scowled and questioned each in turn, without result. Then he ordered the household to line up again at the castle entrance. The provost paced in fury before the group, snapping his riding whip at every few steps.

"Madame," he addressed Mother, "these children are being stubborn and resisting the law. Command them to tell us where the Hutterites are. Otherwise, we will carry out our orders."

Mother stared straight ahead without answering. Michael's head throbbed with the tension of waiting.

"Very well, then, if this is your answer, so be it." The royal provost gave quick orders to the soldiers. "Burn the Bruderhof to the ground."

Mother stepped forward. "It isn't fair. The Hutterites are God-fearing people."

"Madame, you know the law. No Hutterites are to be harbored on any estate. To do so is in violation of King Ferdinand's edict of 1534. Persuade the Hutterites to return, to be taken into custody where they belong, and let justice take its course."

Mother shook her head and turned away.

"Wait!" The royal provost stopped in front of Mother. "You are under arrest."

"Arrest?"

"Yes, Madame, arrest. We are taking you to prison for disobeying the king."

Michael heard the words, but they sounded far

away. He felt Gudryn clutch his sleeve, and he put his hand over hers. Karl stood with arms folded, a look of disbelief on his face.

"But -- but the children!" Mother put her hands to her forehead. "What about them?"

The royal provost shrugged. "Let them shift for themselves."

It seemed only a few minutes to Michael before Mother was taken away to the city for trial. Without a word being spoken between them, Michael understood that he, Karl, and Gudryn were to stay at the castle with the servants to take care of them.

The royal provost ordered them to watch the burning of the Bruderhof. "Learn this lesson well," he said. "Heretics must be punished. The king has given them every chance to repent. He sends priests to the prisons to talk to them. If they cannot accept the truth, they must be punished." As he talked, the royal provost grew angrier and angrier. "It is the duty of every citizen to turn in such traitors."

Gudryn began to sob. The royal provost turned abruptly and ordered her back to the castle. "As for you boys, perhaps a taste of prison might loosen your tongues."

Soldiers hustled Michael and Karl to the stone-lined pit, swung Karl by the arms and let him drop. Then it was Michael's turn. He plopped down by Karl and looked up at the soldiers peering down. They stationed a guard and left with loud laughter and jokes. "A little hunger will persuade them to talk."

Michael sat down with his back against the wall, his knees to his chin. Then he remembered. Oswald had looked like that, too, when he was in the pit. A sudden sympathy for all prisoners welled up in Michael, especially those imprisoned for following God's law. Was it people's actions that sent them to prison or other people's ideas?

Karl ran his fingers over the wall. "If some of the stones stuck out a little more we could climb up after everyone is asleep."

Michael stretched his head back. He could not see the top. There was not even one foothold in the stone wall. He felt a sudden hunger pang.

"Do you think the guard will feed us?" he whispered.

"Oh, you get used to hunger," Karl said.

The first mealtime passed. Michael did not feel really hungry. "This isn't too bad."

He heard the guard talking to someone. "Where did you come from, Miss?"

"I live here," Michael heard Gudryn say. "I've brought food for the boys."

"Sorry. No food is permitted until they talk."

"But they have to eat." Michael heard the indignation in Gudryn's voice.

"Sorry, Miss."

"Hmmm," Gudryn said. "Perhaps you would like this bread and cheese."

"Oh, thank you. Yes, indeed. Very thoughtful

of you, I'm sure."

The voices drifted away.

Later, a hunger pang hit Michael like a blow. He heard his sister's voice again, very sweet. Too sweet, he thought. A gleam of hope awakened in him. What was Gudryn up to?

"Why, thank you, thank you," the guard said. "I was thirstier than I realized."

A little while afterward, Michael heard the sound of someone slumping to the floor.

"What do you think has happened?" Karl whispered. "Is he sick?"

Michael listened to sounds of heavy breathing. What could have happened?

"Michael! Karl!" Gudryn leaned over the pit. "The guard's asleep and he won't wake up."

"How do you know?" Michael called.

"Because Oswald was here, and when I told him what happened, he gave me some of Paracelsus' secret medicine to give the guard." She dangled a knotted rope over the side. "Hurry and get out of there. The soldiers are all outside around their campfires getting drunk. We'll have to leave tonight."

"Leave?" Michael exclaimed. "I know Mother wants us to stay here until she gets back."

"We can't."

"Why not?" Michael was ready to argue.

"Because the castle -- the whole estate -- has been confiscated. It isn't Mother's any longer. It belongs to the king."

7

Preacher Out of Church

Unbelieving, Michael stared up at his sister. All he could see from the bottom of the dungeon pit was Gudryn's flushed face. Had he heard right? Was it true that the castle -- their family home -- now belonged to King Ferdinand?

"You mean you can't live here any longer?" Karl asked.

"Everything belongs to the king." Gudryn lowered a knotted rope. "Hurry up. We've got to leave before the guard wakes."

Michael gave the rope a trial tug, not sure whether Gudryn had fastened it securely on the other end.

"Hurry up. We've got to leave before the guard awakes," Gudryn said as Michael scrambled quickly out of the dungeon.

"I wound it around the chopping block," she assured him.

The boys hoisted themselves up. Karl had difficulty wrapping his thin legs around the rope. "It's because I had rickets when I was little," he explained, "but then so did Paracelsus."

Michael was too hungry to comment. "Is there anything to eat?" Gudryn found bread and cheese. Between mouthfuls, the three discussed the big problem. What were they going to do? Where could they go?

Oswald strolled in. "The servants have all left." He examined the sleeping guard. "He won't wake up for several hours, but you'd better gather up some belongings and be on your way."

"On our way to where?" Gudryn asked.

"Kromau, of course."

"Kromau!" Michael, Karl, and Gudryn chorused.

"Yes. There's a Bruderhof there. Johann von Lipa, lord of Kromau and Schäkovitz, is a protector of Hutterites. Anyway, your mother told me to tell you to go to Kromau."

"When did you see Mother?" Michael burst out. He had to admit that wherever there was action, Oswald was there, too. But how could Oswald be so many places at the same time?

Oswald explained with maddening calm. "One of the guards had an aching tooth he wanted me to pull. So I went along when your mother was being taken to prison. I took the opportunity for a few asides with her. Naturally, when she found out the king was taking her castle, she was greatly shaken. I must admit, however, she regained control very quickly. That's when she mentioned Kromau."

"Because Paracelsus is there," Gudryn exclaimed.

"He's not there yet," Oswald stated. "As a matter of fact he had some patients to take care of before he left and he's at the village inn right now."

Gudryn squealed with joy. "Then we could go to Kromau with him."

"I told your mother Steinabrunn was closer. There's a Bruderhof there. However, my suggestion was ignored." Oswald reflected a moment. "Now that you are sure to become good little Hutterites, you ought to know something about your leader."

"What leader?" Michael asked.

"The leader of the Hutterites. Did you ever ask yourself why these people on the run are called Hutterites?"

"No," Michael admitted.

"Didn't you know that Jakob Hutter, after whom various groups of heretics are named, died at the stake February 25, 1536, at Innsbruck?"

"Where did you learn all this?" Gudryn asked.

"In my travels. Speaking of travels reminds me." Oswald pulled out a pouch. "Your mother told me where she kept her money. Here it is." He handed over the pouch to Michael.

Astonished, exasperated, yet relieved at Oswald's unexpected honesty, Michael divided the money into four parts. Oswald bowed his thanks, leaving Michael to wonder if Oswald had turned over all the money. Anyone who wanted to turn base metal into gold, and who tried to dig up buried gold belonging to someone else would have to be greedy. Still, Oswald had been very helpful.

"Where was the money?" Michael asked as an afterthought.

Oswald waved vaguely. "Behind a stone in a fireplace upstairs."

Was he telling the truth? Michael decided it did not really matter. But how strange that people could be both good and bad!

"Are you going with us?" Gudryn asked Oswald.

"No. I'm a medical student, remember? I'm going to Germany to study."

"I'd like to go there, too," Karl said.

"All right. We can go together."

Michael stared at Karl. True, Oswald had done them many good turns recently, but there was a slippery side to him. Why would Karl choose to travel with Oswald?

"It's time you learned to pull teeth and tell fortunes," Oswald told Karl.

"Tell fortunes?"

"Yes. Lots of medical students do that. You tell fortunes by the stars."

"Not me. But I'll pull teeth if you show me how. That'll help me grow wings," Karl laughed.

Michael understood. Karl wanted to acquire experience. Then he could study with Paracelsus. "Maybe I could, too, later," Michael thought. "Why can't I just say I want to be a doctor?" But somehow he could not.

He waited while Oswald went outside to find out if any soldiers guarded the castle entrance. "It's safe to leave," he reported. "Karl and I can stay with some people I know, but you and Gudryn had better go to the inn tonight and let Paracelsus know you are there," he told Michael.

After Oswald and Karl left, Michael watched Gudryn lay out a big cloak and wrap her clothes in it.

"Gudryn, you can't go like that."

Gudryn looked down at her full skirt. "Why not? I can keep up if you don't go too fast."

"If only you were a boy," Michael began. "That's it! Gudryn, you'll have to dress like a boy."

"But what about my hair?" Gudryn protested.

"I'll cut it for you."

Gudryn gulped. "If you're sure it will help -- but couldn't I just tuck it under a cap?"

"You could, but it would be better if it's cut at least to your ears, like mine."

Gudryn took off her close-fitting cap and let her long hair down. When Michael started cutting it, her tears fell as fast as her hair, but she gamely agreed it was the best thing to do. She dug in an old chest and put on some clothes Michael had outgrown. When she was dressed like a boy, Michael turned her around and studied her from top to toe.

"You can't wear those flimsy slippers." Michael found a pair of clogs. "Here. Put these on." He added as an afterthought, "You'll do."

They crossed the courtyard. The soldiers' campfires had almost died down. Soldiers sprawled everywhere, many in drunken sleep. A guard sat slumped against the gates. His head rose and fell with his snores.

"Gudryn, we can't go out through the gates, but I know another way." Michael remembered how he had climbed the jutting stones of the lookout post many times in the past, scrambling to the top of the wall and pretending to look for enemies. Now the enemies were real.

He helped Gudryn up, held her by her hands, and let her drop on the other side of the wall. He eased himself down, hung by his fingers, and dropped. As he did so, he thought he heard the guard shout an alarm. Or was it an extra-loud sneeze? Without wasting words, Michael and Gudryn hurried to the village inn. When he asked the innkeeper for a room, Michael saw the man scowl.

"I don't want runaways," the innkeeper said. "Go on back home."

Michael held out money. The innkeeper did not hesitate. He took the money and showed Michael and Gudryn a small room in back of a noisy public room. Men argued in loud voices.

The innkeeper rolled his eyes upward. "The good doctor is at it again." He hurried away.

"Do you think he means Paracelsus?" Gudryn asked above the din.

"Let's go see."

They crept to the doorway of the public room. There was Paracelsus himself, leaning against the fireplace mantel, holding forth to a mixed group of pilgrims, journeymen, peddlers, teamsters, and other doctors. His new clothes, a pale green doublet and white shirt with lace collar, looked as if they had been slept in.

"If an unbeliever becomes a physician, he will not strive for the kingdom of God any more than before he became a physician." Paracelsus seemed to be talking to everyone, but in reality he was eyeing the other doctors in the room. "Without God, no proper work can be done. A physician must follow the path of God. If he does not, he may study forever, yet he will not attain to the truth."

A commotion at the door stopped him. Two men panting with effort helped another man into the public room.

"Is there someone who can help us," one of the men called out. "This man has had his ear cut."

The other doctors turned away and pretended not to hear. Paracelsus sprang to the man's side. "I am a doctor."

All three men shrank back. "No, no," one explained. "We do not want a doctor. We want a barber-surgeon." He appealed to the innkeeper. "Do you have any cow dung?"

"No."

"Any snake fat?"

"No."

"Any feathers?"

"Why, yes." The innkeeper ordered a cook to bring in chicken feathers.

The men slapped the feathers on the man's wound. Paracelsus protested, but the men ignored him. "At least keep the wound clean," he urged. "If you prevent infection, nature will heal the wound all by herself."

At once the inn guests started arguing. "Horse dung is better than feathers," one stated.

"Chicken feathers aren't as good as ostrich feathers," another said.

"There are medicine books hundreds of years old. What do they say?" someone else asked.

Paracelsus had an answer. "God is the first book. The second book is the firmament."

"What does he mean by that?" people asked each other. Michael watched their puzzled faces.

"He knows what he is talking about," a teamster with a broadbrimmed hat declared. "He's the doctor who has been staying at the castle where the Bruderhof was burned."

"Ah! those Hutterites. They're to blame. You wouldn't find a Hutterite working for me."

A man who had not spoken before waved his arms in excitement.

Everyone talked at once.

"They are good farmers."

"It's against the law to hire them."

"They're a rabble of rogues."

"How can you be sure there is not one among us now?" a small man asked in a timid voice.

"If he does not carry a sword, he's a Hutterite," someone answered.

"If he does not curse or go into a tavern, you can be sure he's one," another stated.

Two armed soldiers came in. Michael nudged Gudryn in warning. "Maybe they're after us." He pulled her behind a group of men talking in low voices at the far end of the public room. Michael heard Paracelsus' name, and pricked up his ears.

"He stayed at that castle where the Bruderhof was burned."

A man grunted in indignation. "Mark my words, all the Bruderhofs will be destroyed someday."

"Yet they say Moravia is the safest place for the Hutterites now," another said.

"Not in my territory," a third man snorted. "When I find a Hutterite, I turn him in. The king's order has not been revoked. The landowners risk losing their land every time they let a Hutterite set foot on it."

"If Widow Bruhn had not let the Hutterites on her estate, she would still own her castle," the first man stated.

"Did you know she was put in prison?"

At this question, the men murmured among themselves. The two soldiers talked to the innkeeper. Michael was sure they were asking about the two runaways from the castle. Would the innkeeper betray him and his sister?

"Michael, don't look so scared," Gudryn whispered. "Remember, I'm a boy now."

Michael sighed his relief. The soldiers would be looking for a girl and a boy, not two boys.

"Tell Paracelsus we are here," Gudryn urged. "He'll help us."

Michael agreed. But how could he interrupt Paracelsus? The good doctor had turned preacher in the public room of the inn.

"We are Christians and we should live like Christians," he was saying. "It is a commandment of God that you shall love Him. Agreed?"

The inn guests nodded.

"The next commandment says you shall love your neighbor as yourself. Isn't that true?"

Everyone agreed.

"How can greater love be shown a neighbor than when a man motivated by true love finds a cure for the diseases that threaten his neighbor?" Paracelsus' earnestness held everyone's attention.

"Is he a doctor or a preacher?" someone asked. Others hushed him.

"Medicine is an art that will survive until the

last judgment," Paracelsus continued. "God has given us disease. He could take it away from us, even without the physician. If He fails to do so, it is only because He does not want this to be accomplished without the help of man. If He works a miracle, He does it only in and through man."

Michael half-heard the words. He could hear the soldiers arguing with the innkeeper and edged closer.

"But our orders said nothing about a preacher," one of the soldiers complained. "We are after a doctor."

Michael was sure he understood now. Once again Paracelsus was being pursued!

8
Mysterious Message

The innkeeper gestured toward Paracelsus and raised his voice above the chatter of the inn guests. "I assure you there is the man you want -- Paracelsus himself."

The armed men shouldered their way through the crowd. A sudden hush fell over the room. Gudryn clutched Michael's hand. Michael saw quick anger flare across Paracelsus' face. Yet why shouldn't the doctor be angry? Michael asked himself. How many times had Paracelsus been chased out of town either because he cured so many people they thought he was in league with the devil, or because he criticized doctors who pretended to cure but did not.

"Good sir," one of the armed men said to Paracelsus, "the Chief Hereditary Marshal of Bohemia, Johann von der Leipnik, awaits you.

Why have you delayed?"

Paracelsus' relieved laugh filled the room. He apologized for his anger. " 'They that hate me unjustly and persecute me without cause are more than the hairs upon my head. But Thy salvation, O God, doth deliver me.' " He waved his hand toward the two armed messengers and said he would start for Kromau at dawn the next day. The men bowed and left.

A modestly dressed traveler approached Paracelsus. "You were quoting the Bible."

Paracelsus nodded.

"It is strange to hear a doctor who knows his Bible so well."

Michael heard people whisper to each other. "That's a Hutterite." No one objected. Even the man who claimed he turned all Hutterites over to the authorities did not object. "People say one thing and do another," Michael thought.

Paracelsus quoted other passages from the Bible. A teamster pulled off his hat with exaggerated respect. "Teach me to read the books you have read, and I would become a doctor, too."

"The sick should be the doctors' books," was Paracelsus' prompt retort.

"But there are so many kinds of illnesses," the teamster protested.

"A doctor should know the sick like a carpenter knows his wood. He must know the kinds of tissue in the body, the bones, their coverings, the difference between one and another. He must know the blood vessels, the nerves, the cartilages, and how they are held together."

The teamster thought a moment. "If only I had a doctor's hat, like you, I could be a doctor."

Paracelsus pulled off his fur-trimmed hat and exchanged it for the teamster's wide-brimmed one. "Does your hat make me less of a doctor?"

Everyone in the room laughed. "No, no."

"My unlucky stars made me what I am," the teamster claimed.

"Who made the stars?" Paracelsus asked.

The teamster scratched his head. "I guess it was God," he admitted.

"God has given to each man the light that is his due, so that he need not go astray," Paracelsus told him and added with a chuckle, "No more than a donkey becomes a lute-player does man by himself become something he is not."

Amid more laughter from the inn guests, the teamster defended himself. "Satan prevents me from being greater. He is stronger than I am."

"The devil cannot invent anything," Paracelsus retorted, "not so much as a louse on your head."

The laughter exploded even louder than before. Everyone, rich or poor, had at some time or other experienced lice, and Paracelsus' joke caused much backslapping.

During the hubbub, two more inn guests, quiet young men dressed in simple clothes, carrying neither sword nor dagger, came in and registered for the night. The lone Hutterite already in the room went up to the newcomers immediately.

"Who are these people?" someone asked. "Are they peddlers, traders, or what?"

One of the young men heard the question. "We are called 'sendboten.' Missioners, you might say."

"What are missioners? What is your trade?"

"We are called to spread the gospel and warn people to repent and to follow Christ."

The inn guest who had not been angered by only one Hutterite in the room now burst out in fiery indignation, "What gave you the right to confuse people?"

"We do not confuse. We lead others from error to discipleship of Jesus. The apostles were 'sendboten.' "

The questioner whitened. "Ah, then you are of that accursed sect called Hutterites."

"Our leader was Jakob Hutter," the spokesman said. "He suffered a martyr's death last year."

From all sides roars of rage broke out. Michael wanted to grab Gudryn's hand and run, but fascination held him rooted to the spot.

"Heretics!" "Throw them out!" "Put them in jail!"

Waves of hate beat against Michael and almost smothered him. How could just a few words change a laughing crowd into a mob?

The innkeeper ran around the room imploring for peace. "Good sirs, people come here to rest. Pray be tolerant. You are all here only for a night. Can't the sheep lie down with the wolves?"

The clamor redoubled. Paracelsus jumped on a stool and shouted above the din. In a little while the room quieted. The Hutterites stood with hands folded and made no attempt to protect themselves from the anger of the others.

"In my travels I have visited many of these good people," Paracelsus began.

"Then tell us why the Hutterites don't trade like everyone else," someone interrupted.

One of the missioners started to answer. The crowd booed him into silence but allowed Paracelsus to explain.

"Because it is almost impossible for a merchant and a trader to keep from sin," Paracelsus explained. "Just as a nail sticks fast between a door and a hinge, so sin sticks close between buying and selling."

"Why do they have their goods in common?" another asked.

"The gifts of heaven, water, and earth come from God," Paracelsus replied. "They are merely loaned to us. Who has the right to sell something that God gave to him in the first place?"

"Then you believe in common ownership of land -- just like the Hutterites?" a third guest asked.

"The land should belong to all, and no one should be allowed to buy land. Everybody should work. Man by the sweat of his brow may even drive away the devil and his pack, for where man is at work none of them can abide."

Michael heard mutters of assent from the crowd.

Paracelsus continued, sounding like a missioner himself. "God wills that men know Him completely. It is His will that nothing in nature remain unknown to man, for all things belonging to nature exist for the sake of man. God has planted many marvelous secrets, like seeds, in him. It is His will that they become manifest through man's own works."

"From what book did you learn that?" the teamster asked in a joking way.

"From the book of life," Paracelsus retorted.

A ripple of laughter spread through the group. Once again the inn guests were in good humor. Michael marveled at the change, then noticed that Gudryn's head drooped in sleep. He nudged her awake and helped her to the little room the innkeeper had rented them for the night. "I'll go back and ask Paracelsus if we can go to Kromau with him tomorrow," he decided.

He met the innkeeper in the narrow hall outside.

"I'm afraid there isn't going to be room for you here tonight," the innkeeper said. "So many important guests have come in, I'll have to use all my rooms."

"But -- but we already paid."

"There's no help for it. You will have to go."

Michael asked for his money back. The innkeeper suddenly became very busy. "Yes, yes, I'm coming," he shouted down the hall. He turned back and hissed a command. "See that you are out of here at once."

Michael waited for the innkeeper to come back with his money. Two travelers with heavy packs came into the room. "What are you two doing here?" one asked, with a glance at Gudryn. "Be on your way. This is our room."

Michael realized the innkeeper was not going to give the money back. He determined to tell Paracelsus even if he had to interrupt the doctor's conversation, but the innkeeper guarded the door to the public room. There was nothing to do but leave.

Everything in the village had closed down. Where could Michael and Gudryn go? Would they have to huddle up against a shop door? Ahead of him, Michael saw a lantern light flicker. Dark shapes emerged from a house beyond the shops and were lost in the darkness. Michael saw the man with the lantern rap at another door.

"Look, Gudryn. That must be the town crier. Maybe he would know where we could stay."

"But we can't tell him," Gudryn said in alarm. "We are runaways. Remember?"

Something urged Michael to follow the man. He and Gudryn walked with caution almost up to a doorway. Someone inside answered the muffled knock.

"Come to the place where you have been

before," Michael heard the man with the lantern say.

What a strange thing to tell someone! Why didn't the man say whose house? Why was a meeting being held after dark?

Doors opened and closed. People scurried past. Michael noticed that the caller did not stop at every house.

At the edge of the village, Michael stopped. "We'll have to sleep in the fields." They stumbled across a freshly plowed field.

"Isn't that a barn over there?" Gudryn gasped. "There, by those trees?"

"Yes. Come on."

They headed for the barn. Someone stepped out of the shadows. "In here, in here," a man urged them. "This is the place where you have been before."

The mysterious message puzzled Michael, yet he did not feel it was a threat. He and Gudryn ducked under a thick crossbar at the door. Michael heard a strange rustle all around. Cattle? Mice? He couldn't decide.

Then a woman's voice sounded close to him. "Why, they're children. Whose are they?"

Someone held a dark lantern above Michael's and Gudryn's heads. We're on our way to Kromau," he explained in a hurry. He heard more rustling, and discovered the barn was filled with people. But why would people gather together in the night?

"Ah! One of the havens for our people," Michael heard someone say.

"Have the 'sendboten' come?" another asked.

"We're waiting for them. They are at the inn, you know."

"Why didn't they stay with one of us?"

"Too dangerous."

Later, another rustle at the barn door indicated the arrival of the two missioners. Michael understood at last. He and Gudryn were attending a forbidden meeting of Hutterites.

The missioners began the meeting by reading a passage from Genesis. They led the group in prayer, and the spokesman gave a sermon on the inner rebirth, based on the Gospel of John.

After the formal meeting, the other missioner read letters from Hutterites in various prisons in Moravia. Michael learned that names and places were never mentioned in the letters, and that in spite of being closely guarded, many Hutterites were able to send letters from one place to another by farmers who brought food to the prisons, or guards who sympathized with the faith of the Hutterites.

A longing sprang up in Michael. Mother was in prison. Perhaps it would be possible to get some news about her through the Hutterite missioners, if they are going in that direction. He learned that they were traveling in the opposite part of Moravia.

"The missioners are bravest of all," a woman

in the group told another. "They are almost certain to be captured and executed."

The missioners heard the remark. "We're called," they explained. "It's our vocation."

It had been a long time since Michael heard that word. Vocation. Called. How could a person know he was called?

Later, at a farmhouse where kind people had taken Michael and Gudryn, Michael asked about the work of the missioners.

"They gather God's people together."

Michael was surprised at how well he understood.

"Why is that more dangerous than just being a Hutterite?" Gudryn asked.

"Because they talk to groups of people, and that's always dangerous in the eyes of authorities. Groups of people might make an uprising," the owner of the farmhouse said. "The missioners go to countries that have even severer laws than Moravia does --Württemberg, Hesse, Thuringia, the Rhineland. But of course, they have to go. You see, people must be born again."

"That's impossible," Gudryn exclaimed.

"It's a spiritual rebirth," the wife of the farmer explained. "When it happens, people do the most astonishing things." She turned to her husband. "Do you remember the letter we heard at the last meeting? This woman -- a widow -- owned a castle, and she let our brethren build a Bruderhof there. The authorities

101

burned it and put her in prison. . . ."

"That's Mother!" Michael exclaimed. "It must be. There wouldn't be another who had all those things happen."

Everyone talked at once. Where had the letter come from? No one could say. Names and places were never mentioned in letters.

"But she was converted in prison," the farmer's wife assured Michael and Gudryn. "Her faith and steadfastness helped everyone around her, and now she has been released from prison, but she is ill."

"Where is she?" Michael and Gudryn implored.

The only way to find out was to go back.

"I'll go back and find out," Michael started to say. But he could not do that. He would have to see that Gudryn was safe in Kromau. Mother wanted them to go there. Would she try to come there, too? Now that she was a Hutterite, she would never be free from the law again. If ill, who could say when she would be able to travel?

Go back and find her. The impulse came again and again, all through the rest of the night. He could not take Gudryn, he knew. Should he let her be passed from one Hutterite family to another until she reached Kromau, or should he stay with her? No matter how kind the Hutterites were, danger of arrest was always present.

What was the right choice? Michael determined not to let impulse guide him. He would ask guidance from a higher source.

9

Sharing and Caring

Michael waited for a chance to pray by himself. He would pray until he got an answer, if it took all night.

Gudryn blurted out that she was a girl, not a boy. The farmer's wife woke her daughters, told them they had a guest, and then showed Michael a bed in the attic where he could sleep. In a little while, the whole household quieted, except for a few smothered giggles from the girls.

Michael thought about his prayer. Should he make a decision himself and then ask God if he had made the right choice, or should he leave it up to God to choose the right way for him? The more he thought about it, the more he realized he would have to decide first -- and take the consequences. How could a person learn God's will without practice?

"I'll take Gudryn to Kromau." The decision calmed him. The next thing he knew Gudryn was shaking him by the shoulder.

"Aren't you ever going to get up? The farmer is going to take us to the next village to friends."

That was the way he and Gudryn traveled to Kromau -- being passed almost hand to hand, from one family to the next. Everyone approved of Gudryn's dressing like a boy under the circumstances. From all reports, the soldiers at the castle had given up the search. No one had seen a girl and a boy fleeing through the countryside.

The Bruderhof on Johann von Lipa's estate near Kromau, a town of 3,500 citizens, looked like a whole town in itself. Large and small buildings were grouped around a village square. Michael stared at the high-pitched room of the community house, remembering that the Bruderhof on Mother's estate had been burned before the roofs were completed.

"Just think! A Bruderhof is going to be our home," Gudryn exclaimed.

In a little while, Hutterite women whisked her away to the women's quarters, clucking at Gudryn's boy clothes. An older boy, Theodor Dax, showed Michael around.

"There are almost two hundred people here," he told Michael. "It's like a big clockwork. One wheel drives the other and makes the whole clock run."

"Or like a beehive," Michael suggested.

Theodor laughed. "Yes, that's it, too. All busy bees work for the common end, one doing this, the other that, for the good of all." He showed Michael the workshops for blacksmiths, locksmiths, saddlers, shoemakers, carpenters, potters, cutlers, wagonmakers.

Michael marveled. "Is there no end to it?" With Theodor, he explored the dining hall, kitchen, nurseries, schoolrooms, and the laundry, spinning, weaving, and sewing rooms. But something bothered him. "Where is the church?"

Theodor pointed to the community dining room. "There."

"It's a whole town in itself," Michael said. He watched the Hutterites at work. Everyone seemed busy, happy, and unhurried.

"Some of us work out of the Bruderhof for the lords of estates," Theodor explained, "but all the money earned is turned over to the vorsteher. That's the bishop."

Michael remembered the money sewn in his clothes. Should he turn it over? But what if he would need it to go to Southern Moravia where Mother was? He couldn't bring himself to mention the money.

"Sharing and caring -- that's the idea of a Bruderhof," Theodor went on. "It's brotherly love by overcoming selfishness. God's Word would not be so difficult to carry out if there were no human selfishness."

An impulse struck Michael like lightning. He showed Theodor his money. Together they went to the bishop, and Michael turned over all his money to the community. He was not too surprised to learn that Gudryn had already turned hers in.

Later, Michael thought about his impulse to share. How strange! Could a person be tempted to do the right thing? If unselfish impulses were channeled to the knowledge of God's will, what power for good there would be in the world. The thought excited him.

"Everyone has to learn a craft here, you know," Theodor told him later.

"But what if --" Michael checked himself. He wasn't going to start an argument when the Hutterites had welcomed Gudryn and him so unselfishly -- sharing and caring. He had wanted to say, "But what if you want to become a doctor?" He could not say it yet. There was still something inside him that was not quite sure, both a yes and a no. He could not understand it. "What am I supposed to do?" he asked instead.

"You can try out anything you like and see whether you want to make it your craft." Theodor himself worked in the bishop's office, copy-

Michael and Gudryn found everyone busy at work in the Hutterite colony. There were blacksmiths, wagonmakers, shoemakers, and something for everyone to do.

ing letters brought by messengers from Hutterites all over the country, in prison and out. "You're too old for school." Hutterite boys left the schoolroom at the age of twelve, trying various crafts until they found one they liked.

Somehow Michael could not admit that he would like to work in the bishop's office, too. He could read and write -- but how could he keep up with an older boy like Theodor?

"I'll try pottery making," he decided. Theodor left him with a group of men in the pottery shop. The kiln hummed nearby.

Michael picked up a double handful of damp clay and stared at it. How could he ever shape it? He glanced at the man beside him, an experienced potter, Michael realized at once. The potter twirled clay between his hands until a long round ribbon dropped between his knees. The potter coiled the ribbon around and around, each coil on succeeding coil until he had a round, empty tunnel of clay. In a swift motion, he scooped up the loops, pressed them together, and shaved off the sides with a sharpened, flat-edged knife.

Michael sighed. Would he be willing to sit day after day all his life long twirling clay into loops? He watched the potters, his own hands quiet. A woman on her way to the community kitchen looked at him, smiled, and shook her head. Michael sighed again. He would be in for motherly advice. The Hutterites, he discovered, did not like to see anyone idle. Not that they really pushed anyone, or nagged, or scolded. He had to admit they were calm and cheerful. But everyone seemed to know what his job was. How could everyone be so sure?

"You do not have to stay with the potters," the woman told him later. "Each person has to find his own vocation."

Vocation! Again, that word!

"Your vocation comes from within you," the woman added. "Ask God for help."

When he was alone for a moment, Michael asked a very simple prayer. This time he could not make a choice first. It was not a matter of choosing between two things. "God, what do You want me to do?"

Somehow, the prayer helped. He looked at the Hutterites differently. Old Walther, for example, who so cheerfully shod the horses; young Andreas, who hummed under his breath while sitting cross-legged stitching hoods and coats for the community. Women had their special work, too. Some were always in the kitchen, others at the looms spinning, still others with the children in the nursery, or at someone's sickbed.

Should he work in the fields? Michael went out day after day and sowed seed with a group of Hutterites. He enjoyed the work, but could he do this his whole life, day after day? What gave people the willingness to follow certain tasks for a lifetime? How did they know how to choose? The question gnawed at him.

"He broods too much, that boy," he heard a Hutterite leader remark a few weeks later.

More and more, Michael respected the goal of the Hutterites. They made Christian love real. Gudryn, too, was impressed.

"They start learning about God in kindergarten," she told him. "Imagine! At the age of two, when they start Little School. And it doesn't matter whose children are whose. All the teachers treat the children as if they were their own."

Michael wondered about two-year-olds. "What can they learn?"

"To love the Lord, to pray, and not to become self-willed."

The Hutterites had rules for every detail of living. When they ate, the men sat at the right and the women at the left. Children ate afterward. In church services, the preacher came into the room first, then the officers, the men, women, and children. After the service the children, who sat in front, boys separate from girls, went out first and the minister came last.

One day an important meeting took place in the dining hall. the bishop explained that an important man had asked for a refuge in the Bruderhof while he completed certain writings.

"Shall we offer Dr. von Hohenheim a place in our community? He has done much good in the world, both as a doctor and as a God-fearing man who has often stood by our side in spirit."

"Is he not under the protection of the Chief Marshal, Johann von der Leipnik?" an elder asked.

"The marshal is on his deathbed. But he is not the cause of the good doctor's troubles. There have been jealous actions on the part of the court doctors."

Michael sighed. Paracelsus had probably let impatience run away with his tongue and aroused the wrath of envious people because of his new ways of treating sick people. The quiet Hutterites would never stir Paracelsus to make the biting remarks he was capable of making when people did not want to hear the truth.

"We can learn from him, and God willing, he can learn from us, too," the Hutterites decided.

The unanimous agreement to have the doctor come made Michael exult. At least one place in the world welcomed Paracelsus' genius as a physician.

When Paracelsus arrived, his clothes were not quite rags, but they soon would be. He had enough money to hire a secretary to take down the dictation of the third volume of his "Greater Surgery" book, the first book of "Philosophiae Sagax," and the German edition of "Seven Defences."

Theodor, Michael's Hutterite friend, was chosen to help.

"That's what I want to do, too," Michael announced. After that, he sat with Theodor every day, his pen racing over his paper. Paracelsus paced up and down dictating his discoveries, sometimes stuttering, not in anger but because his ideas came so fast.

"He dictates so fast only a galloping horse could keep up with him," Theodor complained in a mild tone, but he admitted he was glad to be helping with such important books. "If you want to be a doctor, though, all you would have to do is read the books."

Paracelsus heard the remark. "Reading never made a physician," he declared. "I began my studies by imagining that there was not a single teacher in the world capable of teaching it to me, but that I had to acquire it myself. It was the book of nature, written by the finger of God, which I studied -- not those of the scribblers, for each scribbler writes down the rubbish that may be found in his head. Who can sift the true from the false?"

Paracelsus kept on treating the marshal. Again and again he would return to the Bruderhof raging against the medical ignorance which had left the marshal helpless. "The doctors cry out against me because I wound them. It is a sign that they themselves are sick. The marshal would give all his wealth to be cured, yet he has been surrounded by doctors who wear silken cloth, rings, and are full of empty boasts." He explained that the marshal suffered from four internal and several external maladies. "All I can do is lessen the violence," Paracelsus said, shaking his head.

At the end of the summer Paracelsus explained to the Hutterites that he had asked Johann von der Leipnik for permission to go to Vienna to see about the publishing of his books. He left by horseback by the valley of the March to Pressburg.

"They gave him a big feast there," Michael told Gudryn. He was now helping Theodor copy letters in the bishop's office. Someone had sent back a report about the honors heaped on Paracelsus.

Other news came by messengers from Vienna. "The doctors wouldn't see him," Michael reported to Gudryn. "The townspeople did, though, and King Ferdinand sent for him twice to meet the court doctors."

"Did he go?" Gudryn asked.

"No. He said he didn't want their knowledge, and they didn't want his. No one wants to publish his books." Michael thought often of how strange life was. Why was everything so hard? Here was Paracelsus, who followed God's law, who cured people with his new medicines. Why did people turn against him?

The bishop comforted Michael. "To live without sin is impossible. That is all the more reason why we must never slacken in our faith. God gives us life to test our worthiness."

Michael agreed and applied himself with a zeal he didn't have before in copying letters to be sent out to Hutterites in different parts of the country. The Hutterites kept records of the weather, the prices of farm products, and the speeches of the elders, but Michael was most interested in the letters that came to the Bruderhof. Sometime there would be a letter about Mother. He would know it, even if no names were mentioned.

When he had time, Michael read the leatherbound manuscripts of letters and learned more and more about the Hutterites. Only two years before, at Schäkovitz, a half mile south of Auspitz, brethren had been driven from their Bruderhof. They had to camp with their children and their sick at the village of Starnitz. Other Bruderhofs had been built. In place of imprisoned or executed leaders, new ones rose up -- Peter Riedemann, Ulrich Stadler, Leonhard Lochmaier, Hans Amon. Michael studied the records over and over.

"So much studying may be a hindrance to faith," the bishop warned Michael in a kind way.

Then a letter brought the news Michael had been waiting for. The woman who had lost castle and children but lived in unswerving faith was now living in the Bruderhof at Steinabrunn. No names were mentioned, but Michael knew it was Mother.

"I'm going to find her," he told Gudryn. "But it will be best for you to stay here, and then we'll send for you."

"But you don't have any money," Gudryn said. "How will you travel?"

It was true. Michael had turned all his money, like Gudryn, over to the community.

How could he make the trip to find Mother?

10

The Swiss Brethren

Michael asked his Hutterite friend Theodor for advice. "I turned all my money over to the community, and now I don't have any for my trip to Steinabrunn."

Theodor laughed. "Now you'll see what a Bruderhof really is."

The elders granted a sum of money for Michael's trip -- more than he had given. Michael burned with shame remembering his selfish impulse to keep his money instead of turning it over for the good of all.

He heard the elders talk about his going to Steinabrunn.

"He will see Kaspar Braitmichel."

"I know no such man," another said in a puzzled tone.

"Perhaps you knew him as Kaspar Schneider."

"Oh, you mean the tailor?"

"Yes. I understand he is writing a history of our church."

The elders wished Michael Godspeed on his journey. Before he left, Theodor confided a secret to Michael. "I'm going to become a missioner."

A missioner! One who risked death to bring the Word of God to people. For an instant Michael wanted to be one, too. Was this a call? Maybe being a missioner was his vocation. The idea appealed to him, yet something in him held back. Michael started on his way to Steinabrunn not yet knowing what he wanted to do with his life.

Finding Mother was almost simple, he thought afterward. There she was in the Bruderhof at Steinabrunn, not far from Nikolsburg and the Falkenstein castle. When the elders found out his errand, they took him to the nursery. Mother sat surrounded by small children looking up at her. She greeted him with utmost calm and serenity.

After an interchange of letters between the Bruderhofs of Kromau and Steinabrunn, Gudryn joined Michael and their mother.

It was fall, time for the missioners of the group to set out. The young men had previously been questioned before the congregation, baptized, and instructed on the meaning of baptism -- to enter a new life.

"He who believes is sealed by Holy Spirit," the bishop explained. "He receives strength from above to do the good which he could not do before, and to hate the evil he could not hate before."

Michael gazed at the young men with awe. How could they pledge themselves to the "narrow path," as the bishop called it? How could they set out to preach to people, knowing they were heading for almost certain death -- and so cheerfully?

Yet Michael knew the answer. They had been called. Somehow, they knew inwardly. What was the mystery of this knowing? When Mother questioned him about his future life task, Michael wished he could answer. Copying letters to brethren in other places and to those imprisoned for their faith was more satisfying than any of the other tasks he had tried at both Bruderhofs. He knew he did not want to be a hatter, like the first leader, Jakob Hutter, nor a wool weaver, like Hans Amon, nor a shoemaker like Peter Riedemann, nor a ropemaker like Leonard Lazenstiel, nor a clockmaker like Veith Grunberger, nor a miller like Andreas Ehrenpreis, nor a weaver, like Philipp Plener. Nor did he want to become one of the "hired-out" brethren, managers of farms, vineyards, sawmills, and dairies.

A doctor? Yes, that was closest in his mind, yet there was something he could not put his finger on. Was it possible to be a doctor plus? Plus what? There Michael's thinking stopped. Two years passed.

At the village on a market day in early December 1539, Michael heard excited talk.

"Did you hear?" people asked one another. "King Ferdinand has ordered troops to be quartered in towns and villages until all heretical sects are destroyed."

"All?"

"Yes, the Hutterites, the Swiss Brethren, everyone."

"Who are the Swiss Brethren?" someone asked.

"The Swiss Brethren are another group like the Hutterites, although many in their group no longer come from Switzerland," someone else explained.

"Do the barons approve?" a woman asked.

The barons of Fünfkirchen had sheltered Hutterites in spite of the king's command of 1534. Their castle, Falkenstein, seemed to protect all who lived in the village or Bruderhof.

"The king's troops! Do you know what that means?" an old woman quavered. "They take over any homes they please, eat all the food, threaten our lives. And what good comes of it?"

"They'll rid the country of heathen," someone ventured.

At the Bruderhof the king's decision caused much shaking of heads.

"Didn't our first leader, Jakob Hutter, call King Ferdinand 'prince of darkness, enemy of divine truth'?" an elder stated.

Stories of persecution were told.

"You know the usual route to Moravia -- down the Inn River and the Danube to Krems?" someone asked. "Bastel Glaser led a group to Moravia, and between Krems and Meissau, in the village of Howenhart, I think it was, he and his group were captured, taken to Eggenburg and had their cheeks burned through."

Another sighed. "They spare neither the aged nor the ill."

News came soon that the troops were quartered in the village. What would be the next stop? Michael heard the mention of the royal provost, in charge of the troops. He knew from the talk around him that everyone was quite aware of what could happen to the Bruderhof.

On December 16, 1539, the entire community of Hutterites met for an important matter, according to the bishop.

"We have had a request. Philipp Plener has asked on behalf of the Swiss Brethren that they join us for mutual help. He feels that our combined strength would make for greater protection for us all in the difficult times to come. We shall have to decide this tonight. We will ask God's will to shape our decision. Whether or not we unite with the Swiss Brethren, God will be our Guide." The bishop's voice was firm and matter-of-fact.

A hush descended on the Hutterites. The silence became so deep Michael felt he was alone in the hall. Then he heard a sound, like the drop of a pebble from a tree. Or was it the scrape of leather shoes against a wall? The sound outside died away. Another took its place. Michael had the sudden impression of being enclosed. But that was nonsense. Of course he was enclosed. The four walls of the hall enclosed everyone.

He tried to concentrate on the prayer. Again he heard the scraping sound. Could it be rats in the building? But the Hutterites were always careful to keep out rats and mice. Were there small animals from the woods sniffing outside? But why would they want in?

Michael's uneasiness persisted. No one else in the room seemed to be uneasy. The quiet remained unbroken.

Someone tried the door. The latch moved a little. Michael knew without knowing how he knew that the whole hall was surrounded by men. What could the Hutterites do? Flee, perhaps. But where? Up the ladders, the rafters, to the top story? And then what? Sooner or later, the Hutterites would have to come down -- into the arms of their captors.

Michael gripped the edge of the bench. His head ached with the pressure of waiting. He could not sit there like the others and do nothing. First of all, why not make sure there were soldiers outside? Although it was against the custom of the Hutterites to leave any meeting, Michael moved out to the aisle and tiptoed to the outer door. A low-voiced command on the other side convinced him that the Hutterites were surrounded.

"Knock first and demand entrance." Michael recognized the voice of the royal provost.

"What if they don't say anything?" another man asked.

"Then break in."

Michael curbed an impulse to shout a warning to the Hutterites, proud that in a time of danger he could control himself. At least he could warn the bishop. Michael tiptoed down the aisle to the bishop, who knelt with his hand over his forehead, his elbow on one knee.

"The king's soldiers are outside," he whispered.

"I know." The bishop did not move.

"What shall we do?"

"Do nothing."

Michael went back to his place. No one else had so much as raised his head, not even the children. Michael burned with shame. Was he going to live forever with the weakness of yielding to self-centered impulses? After all, wasn't it his own safety he was worried about? He must learn to leave all in God's hand.

A terrible rattle shook the heavy outer door. "Open, in the king's name," a man thundered.

The bishop rose, slowly, carefully. "My brothers and sisters, our hour has come. Open the door."

The doorkeeper obeyed without haste or nervousness. Soldiers poured in, divided ranks, and lined the hall.

The royal provost marched down the aisle, followed by more soldiers with drawn swords.

"In the name of Ferdinand, King of Bohemia, I arrest everyone in this hall." The royal provost raised his sword high. Soldiers braced themselves with swords waist high.

"Very well," the bishop replied.

The soldiers shuffled, their faces puzzled and disbelieving.

"What is the procedure now?" the bishop asked in a conversational tone.

The royal provost cleared his throat. "You realize that all heretical sects must be punished. Our great and good king, in his mercy, however, has decreed that those who return to the true church will be given justice." The royal provost cleared a space. "The king's loyal subjects will now step to the center."

No one moved.

The royal provost glared. His voice became harsh. "The list," he told an assistant.

The assistant unrolled a long paper, and the royal provost called out the first of the names. "Kaspar Braitmichel."

"Here."

"Kaspar Schneider."

Kaspar Braitmichel answered again. A soldier slapped him, and Kaspar tottered, his hands to his eyes. Michael's heart ached. Kaspar was not a strong man, and his eyes were weak.

"Why do you answer for another?" the royal

provost asked harshly.

"I am sometimes called Schneider because I am a tailor."

Other names were called. Mathes Legeder. Gutenhenn Hans. Michel Blauer. Michel Kramer. Stoffel Aschelberger. The list went on and on. When the royal provost came to Mother's name, he stopped, stared, and scowled. He rounded up Michael and Gudryn, put them to one side, and paced up and down, as he had months before at the castle.

"So it is not enough that you have lost your castle and your lands," he told Mother. "You have not yet learned to obey the king's law. You insist on becoming a heretic, and you have misled your children, too. Well, we shall see if there are not other ways to make you see the truth." With a wave of his hand he motioned for chains to be brought.

"These people are dangerous. Chain them all."

The Hutterites submitted in silence. The only sound in the hall aside from the mutters of the soldiers was the clank of the chains. When his turn came, he held out his hands, felt the bite of cold metal, and determined not to let one word of complaint slip past his lips. The test of faith! How often he had heard the Hutterite leaders talk of it. If the group had not been considering the help they might give to the Swiss Brethren, would this capture have taken place?

Michael answered his own question. The Swiss

Brethren were not to blame.

The royal provost counted the prisoners — one hundred and thirty-six.

A soldier sang out, "Sir, they are ready."

"Take them to Falkenstein castle," the royal provost ordered.

A strange thrill ran through Michael. Mother had known imprisonment before, yet knowingly risked it again. Now he and Gudryn would share prison life with her.

11

Trial of Faith

Outside, in the cold night air, the soldiers chosen as guards lined up the Hutterites, women in one group, men in the other. By the flickering yellow light of torches, the guards checked the chains by ramming their fists onto the loops linking one person to another. An involuntary moan of pain escaped the lips of one woman. Others murmured words of comfort and reassurance. Then silence fell over the group, angering the guards. They exchanged jibes as if to cover up their guilt.

"Did you know the Hutterites have bought all the crops in Moravia?" a guard called out.

"Yes, and they've spoiled all the trades and rob people with the prices they charge," another answered.

"They have the best farms, the best horses, and ride around like lords."

"To say nothing of the gold they have buried in secret places."

"Yes, yes," other guards chimed in.

Michael heard the swish of a whip.

"Tell us where your gold is," a guard shouted.

None of the Hutterites answered.

"They'll talk later," the guards told one another, urging the prisoners to move faster.

On the march to the castle, Michael stumbled several times. It was hard to keep in step. If he went too fast, the person behind him tripped. If he slowed, the person in front was caught off balance. After a while, a kind of rhythm established itself in the group. Michael remembered what Paracelsus had said once. "It is in his distress that a man is tested, and then his nature is revealed. For in extremity, things become visible and reveal their nature. Then we can say: he is an upright man, a steadfast man, a faithful man."

Michael found himself marching to the last phrases. "An upright man, a steadfast man, a faithful man," he chanted to himself, but he could not forget the chains. They weighed him down. Every step became an effort. Would this march last forever? He wanted to stop, to catch his breath, but the marcher behind him and the marcher ahead kept on. If Michael stopped, everyone in the line would suffer.

He tried to think of other things -- of the free people in the village, who would rise in the morning, go to market, grow crops, live out their lives day after day. They must be the happiest people in the world, he decided. But what about the diseases and miseries they suffered. Was that freedom?

"Hurry up, there," a guard growled in his ear. "Do you think we have all night?"

"Let's get them bedded down," another added.

"We get our pay tomorrow."

"Only if we have these heretics in their new homes," still another put in.

The mocking, hateful tone thrust Michael into a despair as black as the night. The man ahead of him started a hymn almost under his breath. One by one other Hutterites joined in. Stronger and stronger the chorus swelled. The sounds flooded Michael's whole being. He was being washed, cleansed, in a burst of joy. His chains no longer weighed him down.

Free! He was free -- in spirit! Free with these others of like mind. God was with them. His truth had set them free. In that split second, with the hymn of the Hutterites resounding in his ears, Michael experienced the quickening of God's Spirit within him, knew and understood his mission in life, knew and accepted his commitment to spread God's Word -- as a medical missioner! A doctor. A preacher. A "medical missionary"! Both were his vocation.

The moment of revelation passed. Once more the chains bit his flesh. But Michael knew he would never forget the call.

Guards ran up and down the lines, hitting the Hutterites with the broad side of their swords.

"Stop that infernal singing, or worse will happen to you," they shouted.

"Don't kill anyone," others warned. "The king wants them to be converted."

At Falkenstein castle the guards herded the prisoners across the drawbridge, past the guard towers, over the courtyard and into the dungeon cells, women in some and men in others. The iron gates clanged shut behind the Hutterites. Their new life in their new home had begun.

The warden of the castle prison, a burly man with a thick neck, went from cell to cell. "If you promise not to escape," he told the Hutterites, "we will let you be unchained."

"We shall accept what God sends us," was the reply.

The warden conferred with his helpers. Michael heard them talking.

"The Hutterites aren't fighters," one said.

"The king wants them converted," another added.

In the morning, the castle guards took off the chains, but did not reply to the murmured thanks from everyone. Village people came to arrange the bringing of food to the new prisoners. Some villagers stared through the iron grates, commenting on the quietness of the prisoners. Others openly jeered.

"So that's what a Hutterite looks like," a village woman said to her friend. "Look at their clothes. That cloth is worth a fortune."

Another woman held her nose. "How can anyone live with such smells?"

"These people are prisoners, you know."

"Yes, but they are not animals." The woman choked and gasped for air. "I'm going back to the village. I don't want to see any more."

One man from the village brought paper and pens at the risk of his life. The Hutterites wrote letters and smuggled them out through friendly people. Even one of the prison guards agreed to send a letter on its way, providing someone helped him learn to write.

One Hutterite wrote a hymn. Each stanza started with a certain letter, and when put together, the letters formed a secret message, encouraging others to remain faithful to God's commands.

After eight days King Ferdinand's marshal and several priests assembled outside the cells.

"You who have disobeyed our king, hear now his mandate." The marshal read the document. "The king grieves to have to punish you," the marshal explained, "but you must understand that his concern is for your souls. Your salvation lies in obeying the imperial mandate."

"The imperial mandate is not our concern," a Hutterite leader said firmly. "We know only a greater King, a King not of this earth."

The marshal tried another tactic. "No matter what king you serve, your country needs your help. King Ferdinand needs money to man his ships in the war against the Turks. Everyone knows that you Hutterites are wealthy and that you act as your own bankers." The marshal's voice became urgent. "Tell us where you have buried your gold, and we will see that you retain a reasonable sum."

The lack of response seemed to annoy the marshal more than a flat denial. He ordered the priests to take over. "I wash my hands of these people. It is up to you to make them see the light."

A priest stepped up to the iron grating. "We are sent to lead you away from error."

A Hutterite faced him on the other side of the iron bars. "We shall lift up our voices like trumpets, for we are on the right way. We have our calling from God. He has taught us not to listen to the voice of strangers. You should rather follow His voice and repent of your sins."

"What is your trade?" the priest demanded.

"I work in the fields."

"Ah, a rude straw cutter," the priest said. "You cannot possibly understand the Scriptures; yet you want to teach us. We are highly learned men and well versed in many languages. We know whereof we speak. Do you think we have come here to tell you lies?"

A loud murmur rose from the Hutterites.

"Christ's narrow path is our way. You will not make false Christians out of us."

"Just wait," the other priests joined in. "We'll teach you."

"You can do no more than God permits."

The priests argued with the Hutterites and coaxed them to change their minds in order to be spared harsh punishment.

What could the harsh punishment be? Michael thought about it, yet without fear. The faith of the Hutterites was stronger than any threat. They sang hymns, quoted the Bible, and prayed. For many days the priests came.

"How long will you live this blasphemous life?" they asked.

The Hutterite prisoners, through one spokesman or another, always replied, "You cannot convince us, for you do not stand in the truth. We live in the simplicity of Christ."

Michael overheard one priest say to another, "I do not think they are as simple as they sound. Listen to how well they defend themselves. They know their Bible."

The others admitted the fact. "I never heard of a Hutterite in this country who turned from his faith," one said.

The king's marshal made an offer. "You Hutterites will be tolerated if you promise to live in groups of not more than eight."

The Hutterites refused. "Our life is a community life."

At the beginning of the new year the marshal returned and once more demanded that the Hutterites give up their faith. When they refused, the marshal shouted, "Then I shall see to it that you receive the punishment you deserve." He gestured to an assistant with a record book. "I shall call the roll of all the men here. If anyone refuses to give up his heretical beliefs, he will be sent to Trieste."

"Trieste" meant no more to Michael than the name of a city. He heard the Hutterites nearest him gasp. The city of Trieste meant something special — and sinister.

After the first gasp of surprise, the Hutterites waited in silence while their names were called. Each in turn refused to give up his faith. Michael did not hesitate when it was his turn. What was the punishment going to be in the distant city of Trieste?

The marshal slammed the record book shut. "So be it, then. Just remember when you are hunched over the oars, it was not I who sent you there but you, yourselves." He added, "Admiral Doria will be pleased."

The word oars brought complete understanding to Michael. The Hutterites would become galley

The Hutterite men were arrested and put in chains and made to march to the coast where they were to become galley slaves.

132

slaves, the oarsmen for the king's warships in the fight against the Turks.

The marshal released the women and the sick and ordered ninety Hutterite men chained in pairs for the long trip to Trieste. There was no chance to say good-bye to the others. "Spare them nothing," the marshal ordered the guards. "They have brought this on themselves."

During the many days of travel, Michael chanted the word "Trieste," unable to think ahead to the life of a galley slave. When the group passed through villages, stony-faced inhabitants gazed at the chained men with fear and loathing. Michael's feet and ankles swelled until he felt he could not take another step. Again and again, at just that moment, a Hutterite would start a hymn. The joyous music poured forth in such power that Michael would forget his pains.

In Trieste the guards imprisoned the Hutterites in a tower by the sea. Their chains seemed like a mockery. How could anyone escape from the wave-battered seawall? Yet the first question Michael heard from the others was, "How can we escape?" not in a tone of impossibility but as if escape was to be taken as a matter of course.

Michael looked out of the tower window. Waves dashed against the rocky wall. He watched the waves far out, unbroken, heading toward the cliff, at the last-minute breaking on the rocks. How could anyone live through such merciless pounding?

"We must try — we must try," a Hutterite near him said. "Better to die this way, if we must, than be beaten to death as a galley slave."

The others agreed. But how could they let themselves down to the shore?

Michael stroked his wrists, chafed by the chains, and asked himself the question others were asking. The answer came in silence. The chains. The very chains that bound them would save them!

12

Mission from God

The plans for escape took form faster than anyone dared hope. With the help of a sympathetic guard, the Hutterites made a rope of their own chains, looped at the end like a swing. One by one, each Hutterite was lowered to the coast over a period of time and in darkness.

When Michael's turn came, he grasped the chain with both hands, locked his legs under the loop he sat on, and let himself be bumped down the wall in cautious jerks. The waves sounded more threatening than ever, yet the idea of being free exhilarated him. Once in midair the chain stopped moving. Had the escape been discovered? Michael dangled, bracing his feet against the wall. Then the chain dropped on its uneven way until he felt stony ground underneath his feet.

He tugged the chain three times in signal

that he was safe. Two other Hutterites who had been lowered ahead of him grasped him by the arms and helped him to a nearby cove.

"Remember, we must not be seen together," they warned. "Each will have to make his own way back to Moravia."

Michael had already made up his mind. "I am going to find Dr. von Hohenheim -- Paracelsus," he told them, and explained that he was going to become a doctor, "a medical missionary."

"A missioner," the Hutterites exclaimed, using their own term. "Is not that what you mean?"

But Michael had arrived at another understanding. Although his call, his vocation, could not have come to him without the help of the Hutterites, he knew he would have to seek beyond their community life to become the doctor he wanted to be. "A medical missionary," he said with firmness. "It is my call."

They understood and promised to send word to Michael's mother and sister when they returned.

How could he trace Paracelsus? Michael knew he could make his way up and down the countryside without trouble. He was now a medical student, determined to help any ill person he met as best he could, just as other medical students did.

Why not go to Villach, first? Michael remembered Paracelsus saying that his father practiced medicine there. Someone in the town would surely know something about the family. He worked his way from Trieste to Villach, not ashamed of asking for food from a housewife, in return for cooling the fever of a sick child, rubbing the backs of ailing old people, and even pulling a tooth for a fieldworker with a swollen face.

Late one afternoon Michael entered the village of Villach with enough money to stay at the inn.

"The father? Why do you ask for the father? He has been dead for years -- but the son is here." The innkeeper pointed out the house where Paracelsus was staying. "He's been here off and on since his father died. He's not well, the doctor, not well at all, and no wonder, him poring over his book writing and his medicine making and taking care of the sick."

Michael tried to edge away from the talkative innkeeper.

"Some people think he's a messenger from God," the innkeeper went on, "and others -- well, you know the doctor wrote a book of prophecies, and people say that anyone who prophesies that someday people will talk to each other from great distances must be in league with Satan."

Michael sighed. Would the same old criticism follow Paracelsus forever?

"The town doctors don't like him at all," the innkeeper continued, "but they have to admit he's a genius when it comes to curing illnesses. It's a pity he knows so much. People can't stand to have others know more than they." The innkeeper shook Michael by the shoulder to emphasize his point. "Do you know that a year or so back when the doctor went to church people went there just to jostle and push him around. Can you imagine? Here's a man received by King Ferdinand himself being treated like that by country people. Too bad." The innkeeper stroked his chin reflectively. "Still, there was trouble at court, I heard tell. King Ferdinand promised a hundred florins to help print a book Paracelsus had written. Paracelsus said the treasury never paid him. The treasury said he had already spent the money advanced him. The king called Paracelsus a swindler. So who is right?"

Michael smiled without answering the question, excused himself, and set off to find Paracelsus. As he crossed the village square he saw another medical student ahead of him wearing the familiar velvet cap and yellow scarf. People came out and chatted with the student. Michael chuckled to himself. He would have to be careful that his self-importance did not become too strong. Why should he think he would be the only student to seek out Paracelsus as a teacher?

He looked at the student again. Something about him looked familiar. Not until he recognized the student's spindly legs did Michael let himself believe his eyes.

"Karl!" He flung himself on his friend, and after the first gasps of surprise, the boys pounded each other on the back, talking as fast as they could to bring each other up-to-date. Karl and Oswald had toured the country as students, found out by hearsay where Paracelsus had traveled, and finally caught up with him.

Karl took Michael to the house. The first person to face Michael was Oswald, who stared at him as if he had never seen Michael before.

"What do you want?" he asked in a cross voice.

"That Oswald! He'll always be a puzzle," Michael thought. What a strange character he was -- overbearing, yet capable of good turns; greedy, yet willing to learn how to be a doctor. Or was he still hoping to find a secret way of making gold?

"I've come to study with Paracelsus, too," Michael told him.

" 'Diseases wander here and there the whole length of the world,' " Oswald quoted without a smile. " 'He who would understand them must wander, too.' "

"He has wandered, Oswald," Karl said. "Let's find out what Paracelsus will say."

"You can't see him," Oswald retorted. "He's sick. Too many experiments with his own medicine."

Michael did not know what to say. He certainly had not come all this distance to be denied meeting Paracelsus again. Karl let Oswald's remark drop.

Michael changed the subject. "Where did Paracelsus go after he left Kromau?"

"All around," Oswald snapped. "People attacked him, as usual," he added.

"Was he hurt?"

"Oh, not physically. They accused him of the usual things. Imagine, the greatest doctor of his time, probably of all time! People never understand a genius."

"What did they accuse him of?"

"Said his theory was new," Oswald said. "They said he described diseases no one ever heard of and gave them strange names."

"What did he say to defend himself?" Michael asked.

"Said what traditional doctors can't cure, they call incurable."

Karl added, "They said he couldn't cure all diseases, and he said no honest doctor would promise such a thing."

Michael heard a shuffling down a nearby hallway. Paracelsus appeared, his bulging forehead seemed bigger than ever. His face looked strained and his eyes brighter than Michael had ever seen them. He greeted Michael without surprise, agreed to teach him along with Karl and Oswald, and admitted, "No man becomes master while he stays at home, nor finds a teacher behind the kitchen stove."

Michael sensed two things about the famous doctor -- that he was really ill, and that he wanted to teach them the principles he had spent a lifetime learning. Again in rags, the doctor ignored them. "Poverty is a blessed state," he claimed. "Why should I be a Dr. Simpleton with silks and a gold ring? It is the fate of the scientist, the greater his services, the greater the ingratitude. I have pleased no one except the sick, whom I cure."

The days of training began. Again and again Paracelsus reminded the boys, "A doctor is the highest human agent of God's will to man. You must obey the teachings of Christ first of all. Did not Christ make the healing of sick minds and bodies a paramount duty?"

When Oswald learned of Michael's decision, he sneered, "Any fool can say he is following the will of God."

Paracelsus overheard the remark. "When we awaken to knowledge, we are not fools. Can a fool follow the will of God? No. God does not want us to be fools, uninformed, ignorant, and without understanding. He wants us to awaken to knowledge of all the great things of His creation. A doctor protects the body in which the soul dwells. To be a physician is to receive a mission from God."

Sometimes Oswald argued that the old way of medicine was right -- that opposites cured.

Paracelsus retorted, "That would be a wild disorder. When a child asks for bread, does his father give him a snake? It would be bad doctoring to give bitters where sugar is required. What blind man asks bread from God and receives poison?

You will not give a stone for bread. You are the father, rather than the doctor, of your patients. Feed them as a father does his child."

He approved of Michael's mission. "It will be your business to understand nature, not only earthly and mortal, but what is divine and immortal. Man does not consist of blood and flesh alone, but also of a body that cannot be discerned by our crude eyesight. Both the eyes of the body and the eyes of the spirit are needed for the full revelation of the works of God."

He insisted that the boys make their own medicines. "A doctor should know plants of every kind. He must know which medicines heal quickly and which slowly. He must know what to allow and what to forbid the sick."

"How can you know unless you experiment?" Oswald asked.

"You must not experiment with medicines you do not understand," Paracelsus retorted sharply.

"Then why are you experimenting on yourself?" Oswald asked.

Paracelsus did not reply. Instead, he walked down the hall to the little room where he had his laboratory, with fireplace, coals, bellows, tongs, hammers, crucibles, and herbs and metals of all kinds.

Later, Paracelsus explained why he had to continue his experiments. "No matter how learned you are, a case comes that puts to shame all books and all experience. Therefore, you must daily learn and observe. You must realize how little you can do even though a doctor. But," he added, "as long as we cling to our highest ideal, we will be happy in spite of the sufferings and vicissitudes of life."

So that was why Paracelsus was always sympathetic to the Hutterites, Michael thought. They lived in peace of spirit, no matter what outward misfortune came to them because of their beliefs. Paracelsus lived his beliefs, too, but his was a stormy nature, bringing him fame as a doctor, poverty and rags as a citizen. God endowed him with the power to discover nature's deepest secrets, and Paracelsus used this knowledge to benefit all mankind.

Michael thought about these matters for a long time. "Paracelsus is the greatest physician that ever lived," he told Karl.

"No, he isn't," Karl replied.

"What!" Michael exclaimed in utter astonishment. "You, of all people, deny it?"

"Yes," Karl grinned.

"But I don't understand you." Michael looked at his friend as if he had never seen him before.

"The greatest physician is God," Karl reminded him. "Don't forget that."

And Michael never forgot.

The Author

Louise A. Vernon was born in Coquille, Oregon. As children, her grandparents crossed the Great Plains in covered wagons. After graduating from Willamette University, she studied music and creative writing, which she taught in the San Jose public schools.

In her series of religious-heritage juveniles, Vernon recreates for children events and figures from church history in Reformation times. She has traveled in England and Germany, researching firsthand the settings for her fictionalized real-life stories. In each book she places a child on the scene with the historical character and involves the child in an exciting plot. The National Association of Christian Schools honored *Ink on His Fingers* as one of the two best children's books with a Christian message released in 1972.